New sensations cascaded in Mary. The effect of the music was the same as before, but now it was far more intense. Everything about Giro Ripoff was bigger – their sound, their style, their sheer presence. They were beautiful, Mary thought. They were like arrogant gods, strutting, throwing themselves about wildly, their voices tearing the air as the unity tightened again, linking everybody to each other and to the music.

By the same author

The Outsider
The Dark Side of the Sun

EastEnders Novels

Home Fires Burning
Swings and Roundabouts
Good Intentions
The Flower of Albert Square
Blind Spots
Hopes and Horizons
The Baffled Heart

HUGH MILLER

Growing Wild

EastEnders – Book 8

By arrangement with the
British Broadcasting Corporation

GRAFTON BOOKS
A Division of the Collins Publishing Group

LONDON GLASGOW
TORONTO SYDNEY AUCKLAND

Grafton Books
A Division of the Collins Publishing Group
8 Grafton Street, London W1X 3LA

A Grafton Paperback Original 1987

By arrangement with BBC Publications, a division of BBC
Enterprises Limited.
EASTENDERS is a trademark of the British Broadcasting
Corporation.

ISBN 0-586-07224-1

Printed and bound in Great Britain by
Collins, Glasgow

Set in Times

1

The boy groaned against Mary's ear and went motionless,
pinning her to the wall, making it hard for her to breathe.
He stayed like that for nearly a minute, then abruptly he
moved back. In the shadows of the outbuilding Mary
watched him do up his belt and stand facing her with his
hands on his hips. Like some butch cowboy out of a
corny old movie, she thought.

'Was it OK?' he asked her.

'Yeah.' Mary looked beyond him to the piles of old
desks and stacked chairs. She had probably been in there
more times than anybody else in the school. The musty,
motionless air was as familiar to her as the rows of
disused classroom furniture. She wondered just how often
she had slipped off here in the break. One of these days
she would try to count.

'There's the bell,' the boy said, turning to the door.
Mary always noticed how abrupt they became afterwards,
as if they couldn't wait to get away from her. 'I'll see
you.'

'See you,' Mary murmured, staying in the shadows to
hike up her pants. When she had smoothed her skirt and
combed her fingers once through her hair she picked up
her bag, tucked it under her arm and went to the back
door. She opened it a crack. There was nobody about.
She slipped out into the bright sunshine of the yard and
made her way to the main block. At the entrance she saw
Betty Crookes and waved. Betty came across.

5

'What class have you got?' Betty asked. She was in the same year as Mary but in a higher stream.

'Scripture Studies,' Mary sighed. 'An hour of old McGinnis and his whiny voice.' She looked beyond the gates to where Stockport buzzed in the heat. 'I wish it was the holidays. I get to feel like a prisoner here when the weather turns good.'

'Not long now,' Betty said. She wrinkled her flat little nose at Mary. 'An' we've only a year to do, after this one.'

'Yeah. Funny how fast fifteen came. I know the time drags, but I can't believe I've been at St Bridget's so long.'

'What about tonight, Mary? You comin' to the gig?'

'I'm not sure yet.' She wasn't so keen on music as she had to pretend to be. Most of it left her cold. She had never been to a live concert and didn't think it would do anything for her enthusiasm. But she liked being with little Betty and some of the other girls. She would think about it during the remainder of the afternoon. It would be something to distract her.

They went upstairs and parted on the first landing. 'I've got Geography,' Betty said. 'We're doing Burma and Thailand. Great, eh?'

'Terrific.' Mary waved and made her way along to Room Nine. Most of the others were there already, talking noisily, laughing, doing what they always did before the teacher showed up. As usual Mary went right to the back of the room and dropped her bag behind a desk near the window.

Shirley Pickles was at the desk in front of Mary's. She turned, frowning. 'Didn't see you in the break,' she said.

'I'd something to do.'

'Oh yeah?' Shirley leered. 'Who with?'

6

'Just shut it, Shirl.'

Mr McGinnis came into the room. He was the assistant head, a stooped, middle-aged man who always wore the same brown suit that smelled faintly of tobacco. He stood by the open door for a moment, his eyes glittering reproach from behind silver-rimmed glasses. 'Quieten down,' he growled, then jabbed a finger towards a large wild-haired boy near the front. 'Go and stand by my table, O'Rourke.'

'What've I done?' the boy demanded.

'Stand by the table, I said. Don't give me any of your lip.'

The boy got up and shuffled to the front of the class. Mr McGinnis shut the door and went to his table. He put down his books, adjusted his glasses and cleared his throat.

'Now listen,' he said. 'All of you. I've just come from the headmaster's room. He's displeased. Deeply displeased. The focus of his displeasure, on this occasion, is a certain group of roughnecks from this class – led, we're reliably informed, by Mr Terence O'Rourke here.'

O'Rourke immediately looked offended.

'I don't know who the others are, but I can guess.' Mr McGinnis looked at a boy sitting near the door. 'Stop trying to look innocent, Braithwaite. You've been O'Rourke's deputy in just about every act of villainy he's committed since he came to this school. On this occasion only O'Rourke has been positively identified, so I'll address my warning to him, the same applies to any of the rest of you that are stupid enough to get mixed up with his latest round of out-of-school activities.'

'I don't know what you're on about,' O'Rourke said, trying to look belligerently offended. 'It's always me that gets picked on, isn't it?'

7

'I don't remember giving you permission to open your mouth,' Mr McGinnis said, 'but since you have, I'll respond to your peevish complaint. I'll take your second point first – yes, it's nearly always you that gets picked on, as you put it. That's because you're usually the one who stirs up trouble. As to what I'm talking about – well, you don't have the most retentive brain in the school, but you can't have forgotten something that happened only a couple of hours ago.'

O'Rourke feigned puzzlement.

'Outside the boys' grammar school, laddie, you and a handful of others tried to provoke a skirmish by yelling anti-Protestant slogans at some of the pupils. And don't deny it. Two teachers recognized you from previous upheavals down there. And you have a pretty unique description.'

'They started it,' O'Rourke said.

Mr McGinnis leaned both hands on the table and glared. 'Who did?'

'The Prods.'

'And how did they start it?'

'Shouting things at us. Calling us names.'

'Such as?'

'Papist toerags. Things like that.'

McGinnis nodded. 'So you were walking peacably past the grammar school when this horde of rabid Orangemen appeared at the railings and began taunting you, is that how it happened?'

'Yeah, something like that.'

Mr McGinnis waited for the tittering to die down. 'You may think me a traitor to my faith for saying so, O'Rourke, but I'm inclined to believe the grammar school's version of events. You were seen to heave a few

8

soft-drink cans over the gates and declare that the blue-noses inside would get the kicking of their lives at four o'clock.'

'They deserve it,' O'Rourke said defiantly.

'Listen,' Mr McGinnis said sharply, 'and absorb, all of you. This is 1980, not 1690. King Billy is long dead and so is James the Second. I know that many of you with an Irish background have been led to believe that some natural state of war exists between Protestants and Catholics. That isn't so. All that exists is a tide of tribal bigotry, and I won't see it swollen and perpetuated by pupils at this school. Is that clear? If there's any repetition of today's events I'll see to it you're suspended, O'Rourke – you and anybody else who aids and abets you.'

Mary was enjoying the little diversion. Usually Mr McGinnis went straight into his lesson and that was desperately boring. She was especially pleased that he said things in such a roundabout way when he told anybody off. He blew out a lot of hot air littered with big words, so it took up more of the lesson time. It would have been a lot different if Mr Richards had been laying into O'Rourke. He was an aggressive little maths teacher who always got straight to the point. He had once told O'Rourke that if he ever caught him wearing his IRA beret in the yard again he'd make him eat it, along with his flack jacket.

'Now you must all take this to heart,' Mr McGinnis was saying. 'The lesson of your faith, the very foundation, is love. It's a lesson I've been trying to drum into all of you for years now. To be good Catholics we must practise tolerance and neighbourliness. We are not savages. We do not have the right, from God or man, to carry hate in our hearts and cudgels in our fists. Ours is the true faith, so we should cherish it and live by every one of its rules –

9

one of which is that we don't cast the first stone. Another is that we learn to turn the other cheek.'

'Kinky,' Shirley murmured. Mary ignored her. Shirley was a troublemaker, always good at dropping other people in it.

'It is appropriate now,' Mr McGinnis went on, 'that we get down to today's lesson, which will be an examination of the Apostles' Creed. Sit down, O'Rourke, and take note.'

From where Mary sat she could see the playing field. Some kids in shorts and bright shirts were kicking a ball about. Other kids sat on the grass, watching. It was a soothing scene, something to fix her eyes on as she let her mind drift. That was how she spent practically every lesson, letting her attention wander. Lessons had never drawn her. The harder the subject, the dreamier it made her. She began to think about the gig that night. Maybe she would go after all. Except it meant getting dressed up, and she hated going to all that trouble. On the other hand it *was* Friday, and she liked going out on Fridays, then lying in late on Saturday morning. Maybe she'd –

'Do I have to fire a starting pistol to get your attention?' Mr McGinnis demanded. Mary blinked at him and realized he was talking to her.

'Sir?'

'I asked you to tell us what the Apostles' Creed is.'

She hadn't a clue. She could recite the Creed, of course. But she'd no idea what it actually was. 'Is it a prayer, Sir?'

Shirley sniggered.

'Mary,' Mr McGinnis said, 'at least a dozen times this term I've told the class, of which I assume you're a member, exactly what the Creed is. Try to think, girl.'

Mary thought. Nothing. All she knew about the Creed

10

was how to say it. She began to blush. A girl two desks away was trying to mouth a clue at her, but Mary was too flustered to make it out.

'You amaze me, Mary Smith.' Mr McGinnis rested his haunch on the table, staring at her. 'What kind of brain do you have? Even a sieve retains some things. As far as I can tell, you haven't absorbed a single piece of information in all the time I've been trying to teach you.'

Mary stared at her desk, waiting for him to finish. It was always the same, no matter who the teacher was. They would each make regular little speeches about how much they despaired of ever teaching her anything, then they would dry up on the topic and leave her alone again. That was all Mary wanted of the teachers, to be left alone by them.

'So,' Mr McGinnis said, finally turning his attention to the rest of the class, 'I will repeat, for the benefit of Mary Smith and anyone else who still hasn't taken it in, that the Apostles' Creed is the authorized summary of our faith.'

Mary tried to memorize that by repeating it under her breath a few times. But by the third repetition she had forgotten the words. Even if she had remembered them, though, she still wouldn't have known what they meant.

At four o'clock she waited for Betty outside the main block. As usual on a Friday, Betty wanted to go to the record shop and flip through the new albums. As they passed through the gates a boy on a bicycle winked at Mary. She gave him a little wave.

'Who's he?'

'Just a boy.'

Betty examined her friend's face, but Mary's expression never gave much away. 'Are you seein' him?'

Mary shook her head.

11

'He looks nice.'

'He's all right.' In truth Mary thought he was a bit of a pig. Boys had a way of changing when they got you on your own. Some changed for the better, but not many.

The record shop was jammed with kids. Mary and Betty got themselves trapped at the 'M' section of the singles racks. Betty was a Motorhead fan so she started rummaging straight away.

'I don't know what's happened to the charts,' she moaned as the sound system struck up with the current Number One, *Crying*, by Don McLean. 'All that yuchy stuff that's on them nowadays – people can't be buyin' it, can they? Not enough of it to get it in the charts.'

'They must be,' Mary said. 'Else it wouldn't be there, would it?'

'I reckon the kids nowadays have no taste. I mean, look at what's movin' up to the top spot now – Olivia Neutron-Bomb. Ah!' Betty stopped flipping suddenly. 'Look! Great!' she held up a Motorhead sleeve, *The Golden Years*. 'It's an EP, but I'm getting it anyway. Fabulous!'

She began pushing her way to the counter. Mary edged along after her, wondering where Betty got all her money. Her own pocket money never seemed to last, even though she bought very little. Betty always had as much on her at the end of the week as she had on a Monday.

'Have you made up your mind yet if you're coming tonight?' Betty asked as she waited to pay for the record.

'Still not sure.' Although she was restless lately, Mary couldn't seem to take to crowded atmospheres. She wasn't too keen to sit at home watching TV, though.

'Well, we'll be leaving at seven, from my place. If you're coming, be sure you turn up on time.' Betty took a fiver from her purse.

'Here – that's a lot,' Mary said, staring.

'I'm not badly off for cash.' Betty did a slow walk. 'Barney might be a bit of a pillock, but he's generous enough with his money.'

Barney was a lorry driver, like Mary's father. He was nine years older than Betty. Mary wondered if he knew she was only fifteen; with the warpaint and the rest of the gear Betty looked twenty at least. She had told Mary often that she should try doing herself up a bit, but Mary could never be bothered. Why dress up for boys, she reasoned, when they didn't really do a thing for her.

'I think I will come tonight,' Mary said, gripped by a rare impulse. 'It sounds like a bit of a laugh, from what you said last time.'

'You'll have a great time,' Betty promised her, taking the record from the assistant and putting her change in her purse.

'Put on something really casual – jeans, a sweater, you know? If you wear anything fancier you'll only get it ruined in the crush.'

The thought of casual clothes threw up a hazard signal in Mary's head. She could only go to the gig if her mother said it was all right. And casual clothes might be a barrier. In Mrs Smith's view, a good Catholic girl going out for the evening should dress properly. If she didn't, she was probably up to something that good Catholic girls didn't do.

'I'll see if I can make it, anyway,' Mary said. 'It'll be up to Mum. If Dad's back early it'll be all right. He'll let me go. Trouble is, he hardly ever gets in early on Friday.'

When she got home her father wasn't there, but Father Burke was. He was standing by the fireplace holding a cup and saucer, managing to smile and frown simultaneously as Mary stepped into the living room. On the wall behind him Jesus looked down with a similar expression.

'Where have you been?' her mother demanded. 'You should have been home at least twenty minutes ago.' At 39 Theresa Smith had the dessicated, line-hatched face of a much older woman. Her voice was rarely less than querulous. To a few close relatives, her husband ascribed it all to Theresa being an early victim of the menopause.

'Hello, Father,' Mary murmured, taking off her jacket. To her mother she said, 'I was talking to Betty. I didn't realize how late it was getting.'

'Well just sit down there while Father Burke has a word with you.' Theresa gave the priest a dry smile. 'I'll go and get on with making the dinner.'

'Right you are, Mrs Smith.' Father Burke turned to Mary as she perched on the arm of an easy chair. He had butter-smooth skin and a semi-circle of fine white hair fringing his shiny bald dome. His thin, flexible lips were adept at pursing with disapproval, although his voice, Dublin inflected, was never less than gentle. Mary found the overall effect unsettling. 'Now then, young lady. Why haven't we been seeing you?'

Mass again, Mary thought. Her mother was always on at her and her two younger brothers to go to Mass every day. 'I've been a bit late getting to school this last couple of mornings,' she said. 'There wasn't the time, you see, to come to church I mean.'

'All you have to do,' the priest said sweetly, 'is get up earlier. Now if an old man like me can do that, surely you can manage it, eh?'

'I suppose so, yes.'

Father Burke's eyes wrinkled delicately. 'Do I merit a promise?'

Mary nodded.

14

'Say it, then.' The voice had hardened a shade.

'I promise.'

'You promise what, Mary?'

'To get up earlier. And come to Mass.'

'Good. Well that's that, then. Now tell me how you're getting on at school.'

Mary began to improvise a modest success story, reflecting that her chances of getting out, now, were nowhere. Not on a night when Father Burke had called, a night when her mother would be keen to keep her in the atmosphere of musty sanctity the old man always created in the house.

2

Reg Smith had always had trouble with his sense of allegiance. In 1977 he had signed up with Logandale Freight as a long-distance driver; his proper allegiance, as an employee, looked clear enough to anyone on the outside. But when it came down to realities Reg had a stronger feeling of loyalty and support towards his fellow drivers than to his bosses. If a man wanted to keep a job with Logandale he had to be prepared to tamper with tachometers, carry overloads and make the odd unlabelled, unscheduled – and certainly uncharted – delivery to stiff-faced men in concealed, back-of-beyond warehouses. The economic weather meant you either toed a crooked line or sought re-employment elsewhere, in an occupation increasingly populated with undercutting cowboys whose credentials meant less than their ready acceptance of face-grinding. So Reg Smith's primary allegiance lay with his mates; his employers got his obedience, which wasn't the same thing.

In 1964 he had stood in St Anthony's church and sworn allegiance to Theresa. For a few years that had seemed easy enough; she was his wife, so he was required to love her to the exclusion of all others, and to look after her. But as time passed perspectives changed. Reg now had a complicated division of allegiances. Brendan, the elder boy, brought forth his father's fiercest protective streak, because of his weak chest, his sunny nature and complete lack of self-pity. Gary, eleven now, was a surly boy, showing traces of the bully in his dealings with other boys

16

his age. Reg loved Gary, but reserved for him a keen edge of censure and a determination never to let the boy walk on a long leash. As for Theresa, Reg wasn't sure any longer how he felt about her. He did his mechanical duty by the woman – or those parts of it she permitted. Sex had died along with Theresa's ability to menstruate. Affection had been replaced by the dull routines of familiarity. Reg brought in a wage every week and did jobs about the house. It was a sad withering of what had been, but he rarely felt the sadness any more.

If he were to analyse it, which he never quite tried to do, Reg would have found that he had a series of attitudes towards his boys and his wife. To his daughter he had allegiance in its purest form – deep affection, loyalty, faith, support. Mary was his favourite, his pet, his price-less possession. At times it was a hard allegiance to stand by. Theresa had taken it into her head that Mary was morally and spiritually at risk, much more so than the boys. She constantly badgered Reg to adopt her point of view, without realizing she was prodding him in the direction of another opinion, which was that since the change of life, Theresa's sexuality had been replaced by religious mania, and more than a trace of jealousy at the closeness between himself and his daughter.

On Saturday morning, tired from a week's work that had taken him the length of England and back, Reg rolled out of his single bed at eleven o'clock. When he was washed, shaved and dressed he went through to the kitchen to find Theresa staring absently out of the window as she pushed his breakfast around the frying pan with a fish slice. Reg thought, uncharitably but inevitably, how old she looked.

'I needed that,' he said, stretching, trying to head off something he couldn't yet define.

17

'Needed what?'

'My kip. I was right knackered last night.'

'I wish you wouldn't talk like that in the house.'

'It's not swearing, love.'

Theresa picked up a plate from under the grill, using an oven glove. 'It's coarse talk. You know how easy children pick it up.'

'They pick it up without any help from me,' Reg said. He pulled out a chair and sat down at the table. 'You want to have heard what a kid called me the other day when I stopped and told him not to play so near the road with his bike. None of your flippin' heck or that kind of stuff. Fogged up my sunglasses, it did.'

'You shouldn't make a joke about it.' Theresa turned from the cooker with his plate and put it in front of him. 'Children nowadays are turning into savages. You can tell it from the way they talk, from their clothes, the way they behave to their elders – and their music . . .' She shook her head woefully. 'That terrible music.'

Reg smiled at her, determined not to let her gloom wrap itself round him. 'You can't expect them all to like Mary O'Hara, can you?'

Theresa glared at him. 'Is that another dig?'

'Not really,' Reg said, realizing it was.

'If more youngsters took to that kind of music and those lovely sentiments, there'd be a lot less trouble in the world.' Theresa's mother had given her a Mary O'Hara boxed set for Christmas and she played the records at every opportunity. 'I made the boys stop watching Top of the Pops the other night. That Blondie was on. Disgusting, what they splash across the screens for young boys to see.'

Reg sliced off a wedge of bacon, speared it and dipped it in his egg yolk. 'I quite like Blondie,' he said.

18

'You would. Anything suggestive or wearing short skirts gets your vote every time.' Theresa harboured the belief that Reg, because of two attempts earlier in the year to coax his way into her bed, was sexually abnormal. On the second rebuff she had told him he was at a stage in life when he should be losing interest in that sort of thing. Reg was 42.

'You read too much into the pop groups, Theresa. Mostly they're just kids having a good boisterous time and showing off a bit while they're doing it.'

'Sex and violence and taking drugs,' Theresa intoned, 'isn't my notion of a good time.'

'Not in that order, do you mean?'

She stared at him, smiling there, chomping his food. Reg was a good-looking man with fairish hair, square features and steady blue eyes. Theresa's expression suggested she found his appearance loathsome. 'You have to make a nasty joke out of everything. Why can't you take off your clown's blinkers and see that things aren't funny at all? Life's serious, Reg. How can you expect your children to grow up as decent Christians if you don't show them a good example?'

Reg swallowed his mouthful slowly. 'Who says I show the kids a bad example?'

Theresa's eyes wavered. 'You don't do as much as you should. You never – '

'Has the Holy Father been round here talking to you again?'

'If you mean Father Burke – '

'I *mean* Father Burke,' Reg snapped. 'The one with the back-to-front collar that's never had a woman in his life but still reckons he knows a thing or two about how a marriage should be run. He's the one, yeah.'

Theresa spun away from him and plunged her hands

19

into the washing-up water. She began furiously scrubbing at something under the cloud of suds. 'What if he has been here? He's got a right. He's our parish priest. We should be grateful he does come.'

'I wouldn't mind him coming so often, Theresa, if you didn't pick up so much of his patter every time and spout it at me.' This, Reg felt sure, was the thing he had tried to forestall when he came into the kitchen. She was getting to it now. He could tell by the tenseness of her back, the set of her shoulders. Might as well get it over with, he thought. There would be no stopping her. If he put her off now she would save it for later and let him have it with interest. 'What was he here for this time, anyway – apart from bringing the message that I didn't set a good example to the kids?'

'He came about Mary.'

'What about her?'

Theresa stopped scrubbing and turned, wiping her hands on a tea towel. 'She hasn't been going to Mass.'

'Not at all?'

'Not every day.'

Reg leaned back and had a look at the ceiling. 'Who the hell says the girl has to go every day?'

'Receiving the Holy Sacrament every day is important at her age. It protects her – it instils a proper faith in her.' Theresa came nearer the table, hands clenched to emphasize the intensity of her feeling. 'Reg, it's *vital* to her. Going to church regularly will give her a bit of discipline, too. Maybe she'd stop being so lazy. Look at all the nice things I buy her – she won't wear them. She slops around in old skirts and cardigans all the time. She never looks after her hair, won't do her homework. Lord knows what kind of moral state she's getting into – '

'Right, right, I got the message,' Reg interrupted.

20

'She's getting sloppy. I'll have a word with her about that.'

'And talk to her about the importance of regular Mass. I was brought up that way and I'm grateful to God I was. I grew into my womanhood with a sound moral grasp. I was protected by my faith.'

At times, Reg thought, she sounded like a demented nun. 'You never went on about it when I met you,' he observed. 'What did your faith protect you from, anyway?'

'The pitfalls. You know what I mean, you're a Catholic yourself, even if you don't behave like one.'

The pitfalls. Reg considered that. 'Like having it off in the back of my old Cortina, you mean? I don't remember your faith protecting you from that.'

Theresa's face twisted with affront. 'You *would* say something like that, wouldn't you? There's times I think you deliberately try to shake my faith.' She went back to the washing-up water. 'Besides,' she said huskily, her back to Reg, 'we were engaged, if you'll remember.'

Reg shook his head at his plate. 'You fiddle with the Church's rules to suit yourself, don't you?' He didn't want an argument, but he couldn't let the point go unremarked. 'Like when you went on the pill.'

'That was for my condition!' Theresa turned so sharply she splashed suds on the floor. 'You knew it was!'

'And you knew the Church disapproved, if it was used for contraception. so you decided I'd better not come near you. Convenient, that, Theresa – using your precious faith as an excuse to slip out of your marital vows.' That was cruel, he knew it was, but it seemed to compensate for something.

Theresa turned away again, her head down.

21

'Let's pack this in right here before we have a full-weight slanging match, eh?' Reg pushed his plate away and stood up. 'I promise you I'll have a word with Mary. But I don't think she should go to Mass every day. It sounds downright unhealthy to me.' He glanced at Theresa. She was motionless, staring out of the window again. 'As for Father Burke and his opinions, I can do without both.'

'He's a comfort to me, that man. I can't stop him calling. I don't want to.'

'If it comforts you, him coming here, fair enough. But I don't want his tongue on me. If he can't keep his opinions about me to himself, then I won't keep mine about him quiet, either. I'll take them to his confessional and shove them through the grille at him.'

'You've got the Father all wrong,' Theresa said sullenly.

'Maybe, maybe not.' Reg went to the hall and got his jacket. 'I'm going out,' he called as he slipped it on. 'Be back some time in the afternoon.' He waited until Theresa mumbled something, then he left.

Saturdays were always aimless days. Mary liked that. Today, because she'd stayed in and gone to bed early the night before, she got up early and was out by ten. She'd promised her mother she would only go to the library, then to the Wimpy for a burger and coffee at lunch time, and then come home again around three. It was the same story most Saturdays. Theresa believed it, too, because she'd once seen Mary in the Wimpy just after one o'clock on a Saturday and that had somehow confirmed that the girl stuck to her weekly promise.

'It's always nice to know in your mind where they are and what they're getting up to,' Theresa regularly told the neighbours.

The day her mother had seen Mary in the right place at the right time it had been pure fluke. She had been sitting with a coffee, keeping up the pretence of a conversation with a girl who dealt hash. Mary was collecting on behalf of a friend who had been told to keep out of the place. The pusher, like a lot of them, had been tidily dressed, a bit like somebody who worked in a dress shop. Theresa had remarked on how respectable Mary's friend looked, and urged her to make an effort to look the same.

Today Mary did what she usually did on a Saturday. Around eleven o'clock she met up with a girl called Grace, the one she sometimes collected hash for. Grace was eighteen and high most of the time. What Mary liked about her was that she echoed something Mary traced in herself, a desire just to float, to be anchored to no duty or influence of any kind.

Grace was a Punk, and she staggered a lot, which was why they'd barred her from the Wimpy. She was always in the park on Saturday morning, sometimes talking to a couple of Punk mates, other times on her own. This morning she was alone, sitting on the grass beside a rubbish bin where she sometimes hid her stash if there were police patrolling the area. This morning Grace wasn't so high as she often was, but she wasn't exactly at ground level, either.

'I've been sitting here wondering about the winter,' she told Mary, after they'd sat in silence for a while, staring at the trees.

'Bit early for that, isn't it?'

'Got to think ahead, kid.' Grace scratched one of her inch-wide mascara eyebrows thoughtfully. Her black lips puckered. The effort to think looked enormous. 'I mean I hadn't any pad last winter, and I don't see any prospect of having one this year either. The squat I'm in looks like

23

getting broken up soon. I could wind up relying on the odd bit of charity and being let sleep places for a couple of nights at a time, like last year. But some nights you're out of luck, working that way. I near froze my arse off a time or two. Don't want it happening again.'

'What're you going to do, then?'

'Well, I thought maybe I'd go to the Smoke. More chance of a place there – you know, somewhere I can go without having to explain myself, among my own kind. But then I thought, it's easier to get busted there, too. Get shut in a room for questioning by some dyke in a uniform, get something planted on me, wind up in the nick.' Grace pantomimed a shudder. 'I'd go nuts in the nick. So.'

Mary waited for her to say more, but Grace leaned back on her elbows, leathered legs crossed, looking dreamy. 'So what will you do, Grace?'

'Get a fella, I suppose.'

'Shack up with him, like?'

'Yeah. I mean even if he hasn't got a place, a fella's better at finding one. He can muscle in on squats, borrow a place, do all sorts to keep in out of the cold.'

Mary wasn't sure how to respond to Grace's decision. After a minute she said, 'Well, that's it then. You've sorted out your problem.'

'Kind of. Sorting one problem usually makes another one.' Grace rolled on to her stomach, fumbling an Embassy packet and a matchbox from her jerkin pocket. She lit a cigarette and blew a plume at the grass. 'The trouble with fellas is they want to tie you down. You can't bugger off on your own when you feel like it. They've got to know where you're going, what you're doing, what your *plans* are. They expect you to stick with them, like the old fellas in pubs with their dogs. An' they're always after sex. Sex, sex, bloody sex. You'd think that's how they got their nourishment, they need it that regular.'

Mary hesitated, then she said, 'Don't you dig sex, then?'

Grace hadn't mentioned it before. All she ever talked about was music, or her theories on different kinds of drug experience, or the various ways of laying hands on money when you ran out.

'I've never liked it,' Grace said, after considering her answer.

Mary hoped she would say more on the subject. She had assumed, from what other girls at school said, that she was pretty much a freak. Sex left her cold. She had never been able to understand what they got out of it. She had begun experimenting when she was thirteen and she still did from time to time, to see if anything had changed, to try and find out what the big deal was. She'd done it only yesterday, she remembered. The same thing happened that always did. Nothing.

'Talk about over-rated,' Grace said. 'I'd sooner have a good snort of coke any day. Or some prime golden leb. Or a decent curry, even.'

'Why do you reckon everybody makes such a big thing out of it?' Mary asked.

'Search me. I know a girl who believes it's something to do with the straight life – when you're straight, sex is something you need, like houses and cars and stuff. She reckons that if you get away from all that shit, I mean *really* away, the need for sex evaporates. If she's right, it means there's a hell of a lot of phoneys going around with spiked hair and pins in their noses.'

The theory reverberated in Mary like a thunder clap. At long last there was an answer. And it was a believable answer. Mary didn't give tuppence for possessions. She had no plans to settle down in a house and own things. The girls at school, though, were always talking about the kind of men they wanted to marry and the terrific lives they'd have with their cars, dishwashers, fancy clothes, holidays abroad and the rest. And they were forever rapping about sex and what a groove it was. Mary leaned back and looked at the sky. She was smiling.

Reg saw Mary as he came out of the betting shop. He waved to her, saw her smile and wave back. Theresa was always saying the girl never smiled, but she always did when she saw her father.

Reg crossed the road, jerking his thumb towards the Wimpy, 'Fancy a coffee?' he said as Mary came up to him.

'Not in there,' she said. 'The coffee's shocking.'

'Oh. I thought it was quite good.'

Mary thought it was quite good too, but Betty would be in there by now, and probably some of the other girls. Mary wasn't ashamed to be seen in the place with her father, but she might easily be embarrassed by some of the things her friends would say in front of him.

'There's another coffee place round the corner,' she suggested. 'They do nice sandwiches, too.'

'Fair enough.' Reg took her by the elbow. 'I've won a bit today. We can celebrate with a coffee and a couple of jam butties.'

They had roast beef sandwiches and two cups of capuccino each. When they were finished Reg sighed and patted his stomach. 'Magic. I feel like I could go back and bet another couple of winners now.'

'I suppose I better be getting home,' Mary said. 'Mum

likes me to help her with the dusting and polishing on a Saturday.'

Reg nodded. 'Trying to domesticate you, I suppose.'

'I don't think it'll work. I hate housework.'

'While we're on about your mother, love . . .' Reg lowered his head a fraction and leaned nearer to Mary. 'She was on at me about this business of not going to Mass.'

Mary groaned. 'I hate that, too.'

'I know you do. But just to please her, and to keep her off both our backs, I think it might be a good idea to go to church a couple of mornings a week, the same mornings each week, like, just to create the impression of regular attendance.' Reg made a face. 'I know it's not much fun. I was made to do it myself when I was a kid. Didn't do me much good, as far as I can tell, but you know what mothers are like. Try and make the effort, eh?'

Mary nodded. For her father she would do just about anything. She felt he was the only person in the world who loved her. She also believed, firmly, that he was the only person she'd ever want to be loved by.

'And I'm afraid there's something else.' Reg's face was rich with pained apology. 'Your clothes.'

Mary frowned at him. 'What about them?'

'Your mum thinks you're a bit, well, lax about the way you dress.'

Mary looked down at her grey jumper and black skirt. 'I like wearing things like this,' she said.

'As far as I'm concerned, love, you're entitled to wear what you like, as long as you're clean in yourself.' Reg was finding it difficult. 'Your mum's bought you some nice things – maybe if you'd wear them now and again, and do something with your hair . . .' He stopped suddenly and spread his hands. 'Mary, I'm sorry about this.

27

Going on like your mother's mouthpiece, as if she didn't go on at you enough as it is.'

Mary smiled, moving his heart the way she had done since she was a baby.

'Never mind all this about church and clothes,' Reg said. 'How are things at school?' His face darkened suddenly. 'God, that was another thing.'

'My homework,' Mary said. 'Don't worry, I'll try a bit harder from now on.'

Reg looked at her, lips clenched in a tight smile. Impulsively he reached for her hand. 'Bless you, my love. I wish I could spend more time with you.'

'I wish you could, too.'

'I'm always on the lookout for a nine-to-five job, but they're scarce. Any kind of job's scarce. I'm lucky to have what I've got, I suppose. But it's a pain at times.'

'They keep saying at school that we'll be lucky to get work when we leave,' Mary said. 'I've no idea what I'd like to do, even if there was a chance of doing it.'

Reg's fingers tightened on hers. 'I'll tell you something, Mary, and it's a promise – whatever you want to do when you leave school, I'll get you a job doing it. It's the least a dad can do.' The doubt in his mind counterbalanced the certainty in his heart. 'As long as it's within your grasp. Don't go aiming too high.'

'I'll try not to,' Mary said, and treated Reg to one of her rare giggles.

When they left the coffee shop they stood on the pavement, awkward with each other, divided by their years and inclinations.

'Going back to the betting shop?' Mary asked.

'I was thinking so, yeah.'

'I'll scoot off back home, then.'

28

Reg hesitated then pecked Mary's cheek. 'See you when I get in,' he said.

'Yeah. See you, Dad.'

Reg watched her wave and walk away. For a moment he was seized by a terrible anxiety. He couldn't fathom it, but it had something to do with loss. Maybe it was the child in Mary he was beginning to miss. That child was still there, but not much of her, and not for long. He wondered how he would cope with Mary when she was entirely a woman. Then he wondered if he would ever get the chance.

3

'They're a bit like Whitesnake,' little Betty said. 'But only a bit.'

Shirley Pickles said she didn't like Whitesnake.

'They're wild,' Betty insisted. 'I mean they just let rip, and it's like no matter what they do, it comes out as great music.' She turned to Mary, trying to draw her into the conversation. 'You'd like them too, I'm sure you would,'

Ever since the gig she'd attended the previous Friday night, Betty had been raving about a band called Giro Ripoff. It was Wednesday now and her enthusiasm hadn't diminished.

'They're playing in Manchester this Saturday. I'm definitely going to see them again. Going to try and come this time, Mary?'

'I'm not sure if I can.'

'Your dad'll be home on Saturday, won't he? He'll let you come with us if you want to.'

'Yeah, I suppose he will. I'll ask him.'

They were leaning on the south-facing wall of the science block, making the most of the sun in the afternoon break. Shirley had imposed herself on Mary and Betty. She often had to do that, since she formed no natural part of any social group within the school.

'I don't have to ask anybody's permission when I go anywhere,' she announced now. 'My folks trust me.'

'More fools them,' Betty said.

'I know how to behave, that's all.' Shirley patted her new hairdo. It was a copy of Liza Minelli's latest style.

Most of Shirley's clothes and mannerisms had been lifted from the same actress. She had been told, when she was fourteen, that she resembled Liza in the movie *New York, New York*. The boy who made the remark hadn't intended it as a compliment, but Shirley didn't realize that. 'There's some girls can't be let out of their parents' sight without getting up to things they shouldn't,' she said, flicking a glance at Mary.

'Some don't get up to anything at all,' Betty said, 'because they can't, no matter how hard they try. You can't play games unless somebody wants to play with you, can you?'

Shirley sniffed. 'I have all the fun I want. But nobody can call *me* a slag, that's for sure.'

'Then you'll have to try harder.' Betty nudged Mary. 'Fancy taking a walk?'

Mary had been dreaming. She stared at Betty for a moment, then said, 'Yeah, OK.'

They were moving off when Mr Gilpin appeared at the corner. He was a junior English master in charge of a remedial reading group. 'Ah,' he said, 'Mary Smith. I've been looking for you.'

Mary rolled her eyes.

'I've got permission from your home economics teacher to have a chat with you for ten minutes at the beginning of the next period. Come and see me in Room Two as soon as the break's over, will you?'

'Yes, Sir,' Mary said dully.

'Sounds like you're in trouble,' Shirley said as Mr Gilpin walked off. 'He can be a tartar when he gets going. I wouldn't like to be in your shoes, Mary.'

'Why don't you just piss off?' Betty snapped.

Shirley stood her ground for a second, trying to jut her under-developed chin. Betty moved sharply towards her and she spun away, trying to be swift and casual at the same time.

'She's a bitch, that one,' Betty grunted, turning her back to Mary. 'One of these days I *will* hit her.'

'She's not worth the trouble,' Mary said. She looked across at the main block. 'I wonder what Gilpin wants.'

'What do they ever want? To moan at you, that's what. It's their job.'

'I'm fed up with school, Betty.'

'We all are.' Betty squeezed Mary's arm. 'That's why so many of us do things to keep our minds off it. Come to the gig on Saturday. Make an effort. It'll be worth it. After a good concert you see things all different.'

Mary nodded. 'I'll try to come.'

When the break was over Mary went to Room Two. Mr Gilpin was waiting behind his table. He was a twitchy man in his mid-twenties with thin oily hair and bulbous, puffy features. Mary thought he always looked as if he had just got out of bed.

'Sit down,' he said crisply, pointing to the nearest desk.

Mary did as she was told, aware of his eyes marking her every movement. She hated it when people watched her doing anything. She found herself becoming clumsy and self-conscious. As she pulled up the chair to the desk it rasped noisily on the floor. Mr Gilpin winced.

'Sorry, Sir.'

When she was properly seated the teacher lowered his eyes to the table. He stayed like that for several seconds, as if he had forgotten why he'd asked her to come. Then he looked up sharply.

'I'm almost lost for words,' he said. 'Speechless, practically.' The fingers of one hand drummed the table. 'Do you have any idea why, Mary?'

'No, Sir.'

'What was the last thing you did for me?'

Mary thought. 'The essay, I think.'

Gilpin nodded. 'The essay. I got around to reading it this morning. I got around to *trying* to read it. Mary, it's abominable. Terrible. It's illiterate rubbish.'

Mary put her head down, getting ready to weather the lecture.

'Look at me when I talk to you!'

Her head snapped up.

'Do you know something?' Gilpin frowned at her, eyes narrowed. 'You never have any expression on your face,' he said. 'I've noticed that. And now I believe I know why it is. It's because there's nothing in that bland head of yours. No mind, no personality, nothing.' He picked up a sheet of paper from the desk. 'All I can say for your effort is that it doesn't ramble. It's eight lines long. You have great economy of style.' He smirked sourly at his own joke. 'How long did it take you to put it together?'

'About an hour, Sir.'

Gilpin shook his head at the paper and let it drop on the table. 'I asked you for an essay about the most important event in your life. Now, I know it's a remedial class, Mary, but the task was simple enough, and I wasn't expecting any masterpieces. But at least I could tell what the other stories were about. What you put on that sheet of paper is gobbledegook. Hadn't you any idea how bad it was when you'd finished it?'

'I tried my best,' Mary said. It was true. She had been brought to the verge of tears trying to find the words, trying to write them, spell them and string them together.

'What's it about, anyway?'

'Going to Kendal, Sir. When I was ten.'

'My, my. You've led an eventful life, haven't you?' He glanced at the sheet of paper. 'That explains one of your

33

mysterious words, mind you. C-e-n-d-l. Kendal.' Gilpin sighed. 'Have you any idea how much it's cost to educate you these last ten years?'

'No, Sir.'

'Neither have I. But it must have been a lot of money. A *lot*. And for what? So that you can go out into the world a near-total illiterate.' Gilpin slapped the desk, making Mary jump. 'You're going to have to improve,' he snapped. 'I'm putting you on double homework and there'll be detention when you do badly in class. I can't see any other course open to me.'

'Yes, Sir.'

'I also think I may have to have a word with your parents.'

Mary stiffened. She hoped he wouldn't do that. Her mother would never let up if Gilpin complained to her. She would make Mary's life hell.

After a few more warnings and unpleasant remarks about her stupidity, Gilpin dismissed Mary. She went straight to the home economics class and told Miss Dunwoodie that she wasn't feeling very well. 'I'm having my period, Miss,' she explained. Miss Dunwoodie told her she'd better go home. Mary thanked her and left. Puberty had its good points, when it came to finding excuses for getting out of something.

She left the school grounds by the south gate and walked down to the park at the bottom of the road, hoping she would see Grace. She walked round the paths and flower beds and up past the children's play area, but she only saw women and their children and a few old men. She found an empty bench and sat down.

Gilpin hadn't hurt her, she thought, although he'd tried. None of them could hurt her with their words. Not the teachers, nor her mother, nor the other girls with

34

their occasional snide remarks about her appearance. Mary simply didn't care what people thought about her. She had begun to wonder why that was when an unpleasantly familiar voice spoke to her.

'Well now, Mary, what's this?'

She looked up and saw Father Burke coming along the path. He stopped a couple of yards from the bench, his mouth puckering. 'I must say it's a lovely day, just the kind of day to get out and enjoy the weather. That's exactly what I'm doing. But I'm wondering why you're doing it, when all your friends are in school learning their lessons.'

Mary shifted her feet on the gravel. 'I got sick, Father.'

'They sent you home, did they?'

'Yeah.'

'So why aren't you there?'

'I thought I'd sit in the sun for a little while, first.'

Father Burke came and sat on the bench. 'Tell me the truth, Mary. Are you really sick?'

'Yes, Father.'

'I don't think I believe you.'

She wanted to say, *well, don't believe me, you silly old fart.* Instead she gave him her blankest stare and said, 'I'm telling the truth. I've a sick feeling in my stomach. I think it was the school dinner.'

'Then you must go straight home. This very minute, Mary. Your teacher took pity on you and let you leave, so that you could go to your mother and let her tend you. You weren't given permission to come into the park and bask in the sun.'

'Yes, Father.' Mary stood up.

'And make sure you do go home.'

'Yes, Father.'

35

As she walked away, still seeing the priest's disapproving old mouth, she wished fervently that she had the courage to talk back to people like him. But even adults didn't talk back to the priests. Mary couldn't understand their authority. Or the teachers'. Why did people simply accept being pushed around by other people? Why did they fall into line with rules, orders, laws?

But priests and teachers couldn't hurt her, she thought, wondering about that again, wondering why she cared so little about their opinions and motives that nothing they said could touch her. She knew other girls could be cut to the bone by even a casual remark, never mind a deliberate attempt to wound them. She supposed she should feel lucky, being so immune to hurt. But she didn't feel lucky.

She felt numb, she supposed. Numb in one quarter and restless in another. She groaned softly to herself. Instead of wondering why she was indifferent to most people, maybe she should be trying to figure out what she was restless about, or restless *for*.

That evening Betty called at Mary's house. She asked Theresa if it would be all right for Mary to come round to her house and go over her homework with her.

'I'd have thought you could find somebody a bit brighter than our Mary to help you,' Theresa said sceptically. 'Anyway, she was sent home from school poorly today. I don't think she should be going out tonight.'

'I'm feeling fine now,' Mary said, flashing a look at Betty. She had no idea what this was really about, but whatever it was, it would be better than sitting around the house.

'It really would be a big help if she could come,' Betty said.

36

Theresa sucked her teeth. 'Why don't you bring your homework round here?'

'I would do, but I've got to babysit with my little sister tonight.' Betty's face and tone were exemplars of credibility.

'Well . . .' Theresa shrugged. 'I suppose it's all right. As long as she's back at a decent hour.'

'I will be,' Mary said, hurrying to get her coat.

When they were outside, walking briskly towards the centre of the town, Betty explained. 'It's a party. You can nip into our house and put on some of my clobber. There's nobody in.'

'Where's the party?'

'At Barney's.'

Mary wasn't sure about parties. 'Will there be a lot of people there?'

'Just Barney and his mate,' Betty giggled. 'I thought you could use cheering up, and since Barney's pal is visiting and hasn't got a girl, well, you know . . .'

Mary knew all right. She was being taken on a blind date. Betty had done this once before, and that time it had been another one of Barney's mates, a driver stopping overnight. That time they had gone to a pub; when Barney suggested around nine o'clock that they go back to his place, Mary had to decline because she'd promised to be in by half-past nine. Barney's friend had looked very miffed. So this time they had arranged things better. The evening would start in Barney's flat and no time would be wasted. Mary wondered if Betty thought she was a mug. Then, realizing she didn't feel particularly offended by the arrangement, she wondered if she really was a mug, anyway.

They got to Barney's place just after seven. It was a self-consciously bachelor flat, replete with nude calendars, framed pictures of football teams and boxers, a dartboard at the end of the hallway and furnishings that strove to evoke masculine chunkiness and strength.

Barney greeted the girls loudly, flinging his arms around Betty and bear-hugging her, then dragging them both by the hand into the kitchen where his mate was leaning with pre-arranged casualness on the drainer, a glass of beer in his hand.

'This is Jacko,' Barney announced. 'He's in the music business.'

'Hi,' Jacko said, smiling with one side of his mouth. He was short and tubby, with very tiny eyes and feathery sideburns. He was wearing a blue simulated-silk shirt, tight blue Farahs and brown mocassins.

'This is my little Betty, and this dolly lady here is Mary.'

Jacko nodded to both girls, raising one eyebrow appreciatively. 'Nice to meet you, girls.'

Mary read him swiftly. Like buck-toothed Barney he had a wrong-headed idea of himself. He probably went around thinking most girls were stupid, not appreciating what he had to offer. He looked like the really hard-up kind, woman-starved, getting near thirty and panicking about the situation.

No time was wasted on the pairing of Mary and Jacko. After an initial drink – Mary had vodka, so there would be no smell on her breath – they retired with fresh drinks to the lounge, where Barney put on a Police album, picked up Betty and sat down in a deep armchair with her across his knees. Records and magazines had been strategically piled on the other chairs, so that there was no place for Mary and Jacko to sit but on the narrow two-seater couch.

Typical of his kind, Jacko stiffened up as soon as they

were seated. Mary, whose indifference to the man left her completely calm, decided to get the conversation going.

'What do you do in the music business, then?'

'I'm in records,' Jacko drawled, or tried to drawl.

'Oh. Fascinating. What do you do, exactly?'

Jacko shifted in his seat, inadvertently slamming Mary with his haunch. 'I'm a rep, actually. I take round the latest stuff to the shops.' He cleared his throat. 'I've got a couple of samples in the van, as a matter of fact. I'll let you have them, if you like.'

'Fabulous,' Mary said, seeing the evening stretch before her like a protracted yawn. It was desperately predictable. He would get another couple of drinks inside him, he would get bold enough to kiss her, they would mess around for maybe twenty minutes – as Barney and Betty were doing now – then he would make the big proposition. And as far as Mary knew, she would probably go along with it.

As Sting and his brothers in song struck up with *Message in a Bottle*, Mary found herself wondering again; what was she restless for, what was it she needed? Not religion. Not stability, which her mother was always going on about. Nothing at all she could imagine, in fact. It definitely wasn't this kind of thing, she thought, as Jacko snuggled closer and breathed beer on her.

4

At teatime on Saturday Reg brought in fish and chips, as he had promised. He wasn't sure Theresa was all that keen on him doing that, but fish and chips for Saturday tea filled Reg with nostalgia, and he believed he was entitled to his occasional backward time-trip. As the food was unwrapped in the kitchen, the aroma – made special because it included the smell of warm vinegary paper – took him back to his teen years, when he would bring home three-and-a-tanner's worth from Capaldi's and eat them straight out of the wrapper while his dad sat close to the wireless, checking the football results. They had lived alone, Reg and his dad, right from the time Reg's mother died, when he was twelve, until he left home to be a married man. Of all the memories he had of those years, the recollection of fish and chips on a Saturday induced the keenest pleasure in him. It conjured a wistful, cocooning sense of long-ago security and contentment; they had been happy together, Reg and his dad.

'It takes days to get that smell out of here,' Theresa mumbled as she portioned out the chips on to tea plates. 'And there's so much grease. It can't be good for children, all that grease.'

'It won't hurt them, now and again.' Reg picked a loose piece of batter off the paper and popped it into his mouth. 'They used to call fish and chips the poor man's banquet.'

Theresa grunted. 'A poor man couldn't afford it nowadays. How much did this lot set you back?'

'Three quid, near enough.'

'That's scandalous. They're nothing but profiteers at that chip shop. I can remember when you could get this amount for about five shillings.'

'True enough,' Reg said. 'But that was in the days when we were living on six quid a week.'

They took the plates through to the living room and set them on the table.

'Come on lads,' Reg said, 'get stuck into this lot while it's hot.'

Brendan and Gary got up from the fireside rug where they had been playing Cluedo. Brendan grinned at his father as he took his chair at the table. 'I love fish and chips,' he said.

'I don't,' Gary said.

'I'll eat what you leave then,' Brendan offered.

'No you won't. I'll throw them in the bin.'

'Just dry up, the pair of you,' Reg said gently, 'and get on with your tea.'

As he sat down opposite Theresa he looked from one boy to the other, marvelling, as he often did, that they could be brothers. They didn't even look alike. Brendan was thin, with pinched features and big brown eyes that tended to bulge when he was having a bad time with his asthma. Gary was square-built, like his father, with a bullish head and features that frowned easily. Reg thought of Mary; she looked like neither of the boys. If anything, she resembled the early photographs he had seen of his mother. Reg picked up his knife and fork, still thinking of Mary, admitting to himself that he was worried about her.

'She should be there, by now,' Theresa said.

Reg nodded, suspecting telepathy. 'Round about now, anyway.'

'I still don't think you should have let her go.' Theresa forked half a chip and a sliver of fish, examining them as if they might be tainted. 'You hear such terrible things about those pop concerts. There was a bit in the paper only last week, where they said thirty teenagers had been arrested for taking drugs into a concert in Liverpool.'

'Mary's not likely to get mixed up in anything like that,' Reg said, even though Theresa had just voiced his main fear. 'She's with young Betty, remember. She's a sensible girl, Betty. Old in the head. She'll see they come to no harm. And there's always plenty of police and stewards at those concerts, remember.'

'I don't see how they can call that kind of noise a concert,' Theresa said. 'What I think is, the world's going mad.'

'People say that all the time.' Reg gestured for Gary to stop fiddling with his food and eat it. 'Every time something happens that's a bit diferent from the way things were when we were kids, we say the world's going to pieces.'

'I know, I know.' Theresa gestured irritably with her fork. 'But nowadays it's so – I don't know. It's chaos, isn't it? There's no standards. You can't deny it, Reg, they're doing things now that would have been unthinkable even a couple of years ago.'

Reg shrugged, chewing a mouthful of chips. 'They get more publicity, that's all.' He didn't like discussing these matters with Theresa. She was too fixed in her views. Also, he *was* worried about Mary and he didn't want Theresa to say something that might add to his concern.

'They're godless, young people nowadays.' Theresa glanced instinctively at the plaster Virgin Mary on the sideboard. 'Everything they idolize has the reek of the Devil about it. Especially their music.'

Reg stared at his plate, remembering something that had frightened him. He would never admit he had been scared by the image, but he had been, badly. Five men, wild-haired, eyes dead as pebbles, smashing their fists on guitars and keyboards and screeching what sounded like a horrendous warning. Spit flew from their lips as they churned out their anger. Hundreds of young people jumped and screamed and waved their arms, throwing back approval and applause that couldn't wait until the number was over. It had been on television. Just another rock concert. Maybe it had something to do with him being tired at the time, exhausted after three days on the road, but to Reg that concert evoked more violence and devilry than Theresa could ever imagine. He saw something insanely raw there, an open threat to balance and order. But he would never admit the new music and its peddlers put fear in him. That would be playing into Theresa's hands. There had to be opposition to the woman; if there wasn't, she'd have the house full of priests and holy ornaments and there would be nothing coming out of the record player all day but Mary O'Hara songs.

'I don't want this,' Gary said sullenly, pushing his plate away.

Brendan reached out. 'I'll have it, then.'

'No!'

Gary snatched up a chunk of fish and threw it on the floor. Theresa and Reg were halfway out of their chairs at once, restraining Gary. Reg cast a glance of commiseration at Brendan as he pulled Gary across the floor, struggling.

'Don't hurt him!' Theresa squeaked, sitting down again.

'Listen, you.' Reg was on his knees in front of the boy, holding him by the shoulders. 'You're going to have to

43

learn to behave. You can't just do what you like, you know.'

'It was mine! It wasn't his!'

'Listen, I said! If you live in this house you behave like a civilized human being!'

'He doesn't know what you mean,' Theresa whined. She wore her love for the youngest like a badge.

'He knows. He doesn't fool me.' Reg was annoyed at having his favourite tea spoiled. He was annoyed at having this surly child for a son. He was sorry for Brendan, having to put up with Gary when he had to put up with so much else. Underneath all that, Reg had that niggling, increasing by ragged feeling of concern for Mary. 'Now I won't repeat this. If you behave like that ever again, I'll put you over my knee and wallop you. Is that clear?'

Gary set his jaw fiercely.

'Is that *clear?*'

Edward nodded, cancelling the gesture with his defiant eyes.

'Now pick up that mess off the floor, put it in the bin then bring a floor cloth and wipe up.'

'I'll do it,' Theresa said.

'No you won't!' Reg realized all three were staring at him. He had never spoken to Theresa so sharply in front of the children, and certainly not at all like that for years. 'Go and do as you're told.'

Gary scooped up the fish and went to the kitchen with it, his mother's pained eyes following him. Reg sat down at the table again. He didn't want the fish and chips either, now. That one little ripple had upset him deeply. He picked up his knife and fork, making a show of getting on with the meal and putting the unpleasantness behind him. The fish tasted like clammy pulped paper.

As he chewed relentlessly on, he realized that his concern for Mary wasn't going to budge. It was beginning to distract him seriously. He told himself it was silly; she was safe, she wouldn't even have to travel back that night because he had arranged for her to stay with his sister in Manchester. But he could line up all the facts and they still wouldn't form a barrier to his worry.

Gary came back, wiped the floor and returned with the cloth to the kitchen. Reg realized a silence had fallen. It was what Theresa called an atmosphere. He glanced at her and saw the veil of reproach in her eyes. It was going to be quite an evening.

'I might pop down the pub later,' he murmured, giving due notice. 'I haven't seen the lads for a while.'

Theresa's continuing silence told him he could do what he liked. Reg sighed quietly. For two pins, he thought, he'd get the banger out and drive over to Manchester. Which was a stupid impulse, of course. But it was the way he felt.

Sam, Mike, Chris and Dave. The names were easy to remember, anyway. But Mary wondered if she would do what she often did when she had to acquaint herself with more than a couple of people at a time – connect the names to the wrong faces.

'Sam's the tallest one,' Betty said, continuing her description of Giro Ripoff. 'He's got long fairish hair and a beard and his eyes are amazingly blue.'

Mary tried to picture that. It was hard to concentrate with all the noise going on around them. There were a couple of thousand people in the hall, all standing and kept in groups of twenty or thirty by crush barriers set out like sheep pens. Mary and Betty were down near the front, thanks to Betty's determination to get as close to the stage as she could. She had dragged Mary by the arm through a tide of enthusiastic fans, and although they'd almost been trampled a few times they had made it. They were separated from the rest of their group, but that didn't seem to bother Betty. She'd find them easily at the end, she said.

'As a matter of fact, Sam's the one I fancy the most,' Betty went on, raising her voice to make herself heard. 'He's kind of the leader. Plays guitar and sings. Mike's quite short but very muscular – might have been a boxer or something, because his nose looks like it's been in a few punch-ups. He's on drums. You can't mistake the other guitarist, Chris – he's a lot like one of the lads in Spandau Ballet, real mean and moody looking.'

To Mary, Spandau Ballet all looked mean and moody.

'Dave sings, like Sam does, but he's not a bit like him. He looks really haunted. Uses dark eye make-up to get the effect, I think, but it works.'

All the way over on the train Betty had talked non-stop about her new idols. On the strength of one concert she sounded like a seasoned worshipper, full of facts and figures about the band, making snap comparisons with other outfits and defending them hotly from even the mildest criticism.

'They're really going places,' she assured Mary now. 'I mean, I don't think they're in the big money yet, but they're getting the following.'

Mary looked around her. She had never seen so many Punks in one place. She had wondered a few times what she would look like if she tried all that exaggerated make-up and the leather and PVC gear. Daft, she had finally decided. It wasn't enough to look like them, you had to think the way they did. As far as Mary knew she didn't think like any group of people. She was just her.

'How many bands are on tonight?' she asked Betty.

'Just the warm-up, then the lads themselves.'

Mary foresaw a danger of being bored. And the other girls weren't with them, which also helped to diminish her hopes of a good time. She was just beginning to wonder if there would be an interval, when the lights dimmed and an amplified voice announced the warm-up band, Korky's Konstellation.

The blackened stage was lit suddenly and starkly by three spots, one of them pointing right out at the audience. The band struck up before they actually appeared, a raucous snarl of guitars that heralded two men and a girl, spiky-haired with white make-up, clutching their instruments like weapons as they whirled to centre stage.

At first, enveloped by the noise, half-blinded by the light, Mary felt stunned. She was aware of no tune or particular form to the music. It was a thrumming, dangerously buzzing presence, like a segment of a nightmare. She found herself clinging to Betty's arm.

Then it all began to change. As the applause for the first number died and the band slammed into their second piece, Mary became aware of the rhythm. It wasn't just in the music. It was in the audience. There was a powerful unity in their zest for the music. It was there in the way they responded to it, too. The music and the kids were part of each other. Without the words to describe what she felt, Mary nevertheless understood perfectly. To be at the heart of such an event, as it actually happened, was an experience she could never have imagined. Feeling the first stirrings of excitement, Mary also began to know the meaning of holy fervour. This was religion.

Korky's Konstellation played for fifteen minutes. They went off to thundering, yelling applause that sank abruptly as the stage darkened again. Mary felt the

47

tension build. There was talk going on around her but it was hushed, expectant.

Betty nudged her. 'Great, eh?'

Mary nodded. If Giro Ripoff were anywhere near as stunning as the warm-up, there would be no danger of getting bored.

'They're here!' a voice roared over the PA, making Mary jump. An instant later a thunderflash exploded onstage and lights, dozens of them, poured concentrated beams down through the smoke and on to four young men in studded black leather. The roar from the crowd drowned out their opening bars, then the music surged forward, a shattering scream of instruments and voices as Sam, Chris and Dave strode to the front of the stage and hurled their art at their adoring fans. At the back, hunched and frenetic, Mike hammered rhythms from his drums.

New sensations cascaded in Mary. The effect of the music was the same as before, but now it was far more intense. Everything about Giro Ripoff was bigger – their sound, their style, their sheer presence. They were beautiful, Mary thought. They were like arrogant gods, strutting, throwing themselves about wildly, their voices tearing the air as the unity tightened again, linking everybody to each other and to the music.

By the second number Mary was gripping the barrier, staring, detached from herself. It was all dizzying and glorious. She had never known such excitement and for the first time, too, she was watching a young man with open, avid attraction. He was the one called Chris, weaving and stomping with his guitar held aloft, his dark hair half-obscuring his face. He embodied something vital to Mary, something she had never been aware she needed. Until now.

48

The concert over-ran by half an hour. Even so, for most of the people there it finished too soon. For Mary it certainly did. Numbly she followed Betty out of the hall, clinging to her as the crowd buffeted them towards the doors. When they were outside Betty pointed to some of their friends waiting on the other side of the road.

'Do you want to go across, or will we give them the slip?'

Mary didn't understand. 'What do you want to give them the slip for?'

'I was hoping to get close to the band. Even for a minute would be worth it. We'll never do it with all of them hanging on.'

Mary was all for the idea. She only had to imagine getting near Chris, maybe catching his eye for a moment, to feel watery round the knees.

'You'll have to watch you don't miss the train back,' she told Betty.

'Sod the train. I can stay at your auntie's if I have to, can't I? Or I'm sure I could get a lift.'

Mary said Aunt Louise would be glad to put her up. 'Now how do we get a look at the band?'

'Just follow your little pal,' Betty said.

She led Mary along the side of the hall. By a door at the far end there were about fifty fans, being held back in a rough semi-circle by a trio of muscular stewards.

'We've a better chance of getting close if we find out where their van's parked.'

Betty hurried round the perimeter of the crowd, waving for Mary to keep up. At the corner she peered along the darkened road, then pointed.

'There. Under the lamp post. They'll make a bee-line for it. Come on.'

Shaking with excitement, Mary stood by Betty in the

shadows beyond the battered van, watching the corner. They could hear some commotion, scattered shouts and cheers, as a roadie laden with instrument cases came into view.

'Any second now,' Betty said.

As the roadie reached the van the band appeared, half-running, pursued by a group of fans. As they drew closer Betty and Mary stepped forward. Mary gulped, feeling she was going to faint. *They were there, right in front of her!*

'Hey, Sam!' Betty yelled as the other fans clustered round the van. 'I love you!'

Sam glanced at her as he climbed in through the sliding door. A smile flickered across his face. Behind him Chris, carrying a mike box, trying to avoid a girl who had her arms stretched out to him, glanced across and looked straight at Mary. He winked at her. Then he was gone. The door slammed shut and the van moved off, throwing out acrid smoke from its exhaust.

Mary stared as the van rounded the corner and disappeared. Betty was saying something to her, but she couldn't hear. The image of Chris's confident, beautiful face was printed dazzlingly on her mind. He had looked at her and he had winked! At her! This had been the most staggering, fabulous night of her life. She was changed. In the space of one evening she had fallen in love with a band and with a man. And she had found a faith to follow. Mary believed she was going to cry.

5

In December, towards the end of term, teachers at St Bridget's Catholic Comprehensive were required to provide the headmaster with brief reports on their pupils' progress during term. Additionally, and for the first time, they were instructed to submit longer reports on difficult pupils, with a view to providing what the head, Mr Golding, described as 'a tentative picture of weak or under-emphasized areas of educational technique in the school.'

Mr Golding's new directive was variously described by the staff as a waste of time, daft, more red tape, twaddle, and bullshit. In Mr Gilpin's view, expressed to other teachers in the staff room and to his wife over dinner, the head's hope of obtaining an overall picture of educational flaws at St Bridget's showed that the man was completely out of touch with reality.

'St Bridget's is a sub-standard school. It's that way because Golding lives in a world of his own. He sees himself and the other staff as bright-eyed purveyors of enlightenment to young minds that are dead eager to soak up wisdom. He believes it against all the evidence. The fact is we're overworked, under-equipped souls trying to bang some civilizing influences into a mob of near-savages who don't want to know.'

Mr Gilpin's disillusionment, his wife had noticed, seemed to date from the time he was offered a job in a private school, to commence after the next Easter break. He maintained he was still thinking about it, but Mrs

Gilpin suspected he had decided he would take the post. All he was doing now was arming himself with excuses for running out on St Bridget's.

'The comprehensive system just doesn't work,' Mr Gilpin further insisted. 'Assembly-line education, that's all. Designed to produce robots – mindless, characterless lumps that do nothing but obey and conform. Well, I want to educate children to become *people*. Individuals.'

Mrs Gilpin reflected, as her husband went off to the sitting room to write his reports, that he would definitely be taking that other job. She wondered if it meant he would drop his membership of the Labour Party. She hoped so. He had never been comfortable with Socialism.

In the sitting room Mr Gilpin sat by the fire and arranged his notes along one padded arm of his chair. His parting reports would be succinct, he decided, and there would be no unnecessary caution or pandering. He would tell things the way they were.

He looked down at his list of thick-heads. Best to start with the worst of them, he decided, since the worst of them annoyed him most and he could set down their miserable histories with maximum venomous energy. He narrowed his puffy eyes as he made the shortlist. It wasn't a difficult task; he underlined the names of Brian Ackroyd, a boy whose brain definitely wasn't user-friendly, Ray Chilton, the one who listened with his mouth open and still couldn't distinguish between noun and pronoun, and the thickest of a very thick bunch, Mary Smith.

Gilpin put his clipboard on his knees and inserted a fresh sheet of lined foolscap under the clip. He uncapped his Parker and poised it carefully over the paper. He thought of Mary Smith for a minute, then began writing.

It took him the best part of half an hour. When he had

finished he unclipped the paper and read it over. Here and there, he supposed, he had been perhaps less than fair, less than charitable. But he could put his hand on his heart and say he had told the truth.

Two days later, together with a thick bundle of others, Mary Smith's report landed on Mr Golding's desk. Mary's was ninth from the top and Mr Golding was already dispirited by the time he picked it up. As he read, he began to sigh.

Of all the pupils I have dealt with in remedial reading and writing classes, Mary Smith is undoubtedly the one most clearly beyond help or hope. She is almost sixteen, yet she can scarcely read or write. She displays no appreciable traces of character or spirit. In the profoundest sense the girl may be described as witless, and there is no evidence to suggest that her condition is reversible.

Mary Smith's record shows that, although she has no clinically definable subnormality, she has never displayed any aptitude for learning. The faculty is entirely missing from her. In appearance she is very untidy and has a permanently vacant expression. The network of rumour and scandal around St Bridget's suggests that, not to put too fine a point on it, Mary Smith's sole talent is in providing unseemly recreation for older and younger boys during school breaks. While I can offer no firm evidence of this, nor do I wish to obtain such evidence, I would say that the story is easy to believe, since the girl evokes nothing so strongly as the vacuous demeanour of the born slut.

Mr Golding dropped the report. He didn't want to read any more. Apart from the depressing picture it painted, its tone suggested that Mr Gilpin might no longer be the man for the remedial classes. He appeared to have lost his compassion, and his bitterness and cynicism in past weeks had been on the climb. It wasn't easy or encouraging for a teacher to face, day in and day out, classrooms full of slow-witted, indifferent children; perhaps Mr Gilpin had just had too much.

Mr Golding picked up his coffee mug and took a sip, thinking of Mary Smith and wondering what the world would do to her. In the past five years three girls from the school had been expelled for using and peddling drugs; in the same period two other girls had become pregnant, five had been through the juvenile courts for theft and numerous others had been the subject of police interest for a shattering variety of reasons.

But Mary Smith hadn't been in any particular trouble, and although that might simply have been luck, Mr Golding was tempted to suspect it was something else. Mary was unlike those other girls in one noticeable particular – she was passive. She didn't *do* things, she had them done to her. It was easy to imagine that she hadn't instigated anything in her life.

That was saddening. It meant the world might be extra hard on Mary, given that she couldn't set anything in motion to counter society's pressures. And the socio-economic pressures on a near-illiterate young woman were severe, without the added burden of a passive nature.

Mr Golding put down his cup and decided that he would, after all, read the rest of the report on Mary Smith. It wouldn't offer any solace, for Mr Gilpin had recently stopped saying anything constructive about the school, its methods or its pupils. But it was a headmaster's duty to keep himself thoroughly informed of what was going on – even if, as Mr Golding had recently begun to realize, there wasn't much he could do about it.

There was to be a big concert in Liverpool on 20th December, a Saturday. Giro Ripoff were topping the bill.

They were getting really big now. They had cut an album and a single from it was going to be released in the New Year. They had regular gigs all over the country and their following had grown to the point where they were mentioned regularly in the music press. Mary kept all the publicity material she could lay her hands on. One wall of her bedroom was a shrine to the band with pictures, stickers, two posters and a corner set aside for photographs of Chris.

Since the first time she saw them in Manchester she had been to another eleven of the band's concerts. Her adoration had hardened into worship, but as time passed the trips got harder to make. For one thing, her parents – Theresa in particular – were getting increasingly touchy about her making train and coach journeys over wider and wider distances; for another, it was getting very pricey. The travelling wasn't cheap and as Giro Ripoff's popularity grew, so did the ticket prices. For a while Betty subsidised Mary, but then Betty fell out with Barney and the cash supply dried up.

Betty had come up with a solution of sorts. The trouble was that it couldn't be relied on. When it worked it was great; Mary could make enough at one go to pay for new clothes – punk gear, kept at Betty's house – and make-up, and still save enough to pay the fare and the ticket price whenever there was a gig.

The solution was an ancient one. The girls sold themselves to men. Betty had a talent for spotting likely punters in pubs and lining them up, but guaranteeing they would pay was something she couldn't do. One man ran away from Mary in an alley after having what he'd promised her £25 for. Another one slipped her the money in a folded wad, which turned out to be two pound notes wrapped around fifteen sheets of newspaper cut to

55

banknote size. And there was always the danger of picking up a weirdie; Mary had a narrow squeak with one and so had Betty. 'I could have got murdered,' Mary said after her experience with the man who had wanted to handcuff her, and for a while after that she wouldn't do the rounds with Betty, until she ached so badly to see the band she swallowed her apprehension and picked up £40 in less than an hour.

The concert on 20th December was a must. It was going to be the biggest one yet. More than that, the lads were beginning to notice Mary and Betty. Their steady presence at gigs, right up front, and their habit of appearing beside the van – a shiny new one now – had made them register. There was a casual bond, an acknowledgement from the boys that the girls existed. And Chris had winked at Mary three times now. She dreamt about it, regularly. She didn't want to miss a single concert from now on. She wanted the bond strengthened and for that to happen she had to turn up at every gig she possibly could. One way or another she was going to get close to Chris. She was going to talk to him and tell him she loved him.

'You get really determined about some things these days,' Betty had told her. 'You've changed a lot, kid.'

Mary's determination was at its peak where the Liverpool gig was concerned. Even though there were more snags than usual. Her mother had said flatly that she wasn't going. Her father told her that this time he felt he had to put his foot down. There would be relatives visiting that weekend, an aunt and uncle they hadn't seen for two years who were looking forward to spending some time with Mary and the two boys.

'Christmas is a time to be at home,' Theresa pointed out. 'It's a time for remembering Our Lord's birth, too, instead of gallivanting about after a crew of hairy heathens. You'll stay put and try to behave like a decent girl, for Christmas at least.'

Money was another barrier. Mary had spent more than she meant to on Christmas presents. And three days before the gig, she realized she had also underestimated the cost of getting to Liverpool and back. After school on Thursday she had an emergency meeting with Betty in a little café near the school.

'You're never going to be able to go, are you?' Betty said. 'It's all stacked against you this time.'

Mary glared at her. 'You're supposed to help me out, not depress me. I've got to get the cash together. That's the main problem.'

'You could have given me some warning.'

'I didn't realize how hard-up I was until I started working it out. Even if I'd another tenner, I wouldn't have anything left over to spend.'

'Christ, you'd want about twenty for your pocket. They're pricey, Liverpool gigs. There's drinks, something to eat later on, all that. And it's always a good idea to have something for an emergency.' Betty shook her head. 'Face it, Mary. You're going to have to miss this one. Even if you'd the cash, how would you get past your mum and dad? They've put their foot down, haven't they?'

'I don't care what they say. I'm going.' Mary leaned across the table, her face tense. 'Can you organize for me to pick up a few quid?'

'I don't think so.'

'Why not?'

'It's getting dicey. That barman in the George has warned me off, and the manager at the Rowan Tree watches me like a hawk every time I go in there now.'

57

'You just don't want to do it because you're fixed up,' Mary snapped. 'You know I can't do it on my own. I'm no good at chatting them up and making deals.'

'Look, hang on,' Betty protested. 'I told you, it's getting to be too much of a risk.'

'That's not true! You don't want to go to the trouble because you've got the cash you need and your mum doesn't care what you get up to and . . . and you're free as a bird so why should you go out of your way to do anything for me? That's it, isn't it?'

Betty shot up from her chair. 'Think what you like.' She spun around and walked to the door, leaving Mary gaping after her. At the door she turned and glared across the café, not quite meeting Mary's eyes. 'I'll bring you your gear to school tomorrow,' she said, and walked out.

Mary sat for a minute and considered her situation. She was out on an edge. Never in her life had she been so much in need of something and so unlikely to get it. She pictured the gig in Liverpool, saw Betty raving away down at the front, lapping up every second. She was enjoying herself, she was rapturous, while Mary, in split-screen, sat at home in her prettiest frock listening to her auntie nattering and watching her uncle knock out his pipe on the ashtray. She closed her eyes tightly and pictured Chris, scowling the way he did on stage, then smiling at her under a street light, and winking.

Mary stood up. She grabbed her school bag, paid for the two coffees and strode out on to the street. She was going to that gig. Nothing would stop her. *Nothing!* The certainty was like something powerful at her back, thrusting her forward.

Two hours later she was in the town centre. She had had to lie her way out of the house, telling her scowling

58

mother that she was going with Betty to the hospital to
see one of their friends who had been taken in with
glandular fever. In jeans, a heavy sweater and the duffel
coat her mother insisted on her wearing, she had made
her way directly to a Ladies near the centre of town,
locked herself in and applied her make-up in front of a
cracked mirror.

Now, hoping she looked old enough to enter a pub
without being challenged, she roamed the streets looking
for a likely pitch. Just in case Betty had been telling the
truth, she avoided the George and the Rowan Tree. She
stopped outside a place with etched-glass windows and
varnished mahogany doors with brass handles. It was old
and expensive looking. For a minute she was doubtful
about going in; maybe they didn't allow denim. Then a
girl and a man came out. They were both wearing jeans.
Mary moistened her lips, patted the sides of her hair and
went in.

There seemed to be about an acre of red carpet
between the door and the bar, which was at right angles
to the entrance. Red-glass candleholders glowed on the
tables. The wallpaper was patterned red flock. The two
barmen even wore red jackets. Mary made her way past
couples and triples sitting huddled over drinks, their
buzzing conversation mingling with the piped music,
which was some kind of twangy, slow-tempo string tune.
A barman gave her a half-interested look as she stepped
up to the bar.

'A Malibu, please.'

The barman nodded and took a glass to the white
bottle on the back shelf. So the make-up worked. Mary
looked cautiously right and left. There were four men
and three women standing at the bar. Two of the women
seemed to be with the same man. Which left two men on

their own. One was about forty and he was smoking a pipe. Betty said pipe-smokers were no good; they were always settled types, fixed in their ways, the kind who go out for a drink and nothing else. The other one was younger, maybe thirty. He looked shy, glancing at his shoes every few seconds, straight ahead the rest of the time. Mary had the feeling that if she spoke to him he would down his drink and leave.

'There you are, love.' The barman put the drink in front of her.

'Ta.' Mary paid him and took a sip. Turning slowly, casually, she looked around the room. It was a funny atmosphere to gauge. Not like a pub, really, but not like a wine bar or a club, either. There didn't seem to be a general age level; there were old people, middle-aged and young ones in a fairly even mix. She couldn't see anybody on their own apart from the two at the bar. Mary reckoned she had wasted the price of a drink.

Swallowing some more of the coconut liqueur, she decided that at the next place, she would check the crowd carefully before investing any money. Time would be saved that way, too. She looked at the clock above the bar. She would have to move.

The next swallow from the glass was hasty and too large. Mary gulped, choked, then started coughing. She put down the glass before she dropped it and fumbled for a hankie, keeping one hand over her mouth as she spluttered. A man sitting at a table with another man looked round at the small commotion. He muttered something to his companion, then got up and crossed to the bar.

'Steady on, love,' he said, patting Mary gently on the back. 'You'll have to start taking more water with it.'

Mary dabbed her streaming eyes with her hankie and

blinked at him. The film of tears cleared and she realized it was Barney, Betty's ex-boyfriend. She gulped a couple of times and managed a choked hello.

'Come and sit down,' he said. 'I'll bring your drink.'

Mary followed him to the table, still coughing. She sat down and when the spasms had passed Barney introduced her to the other man. He was Derek, another one of the self-delusion brigade Barney seemed to surround himself with. He made a strong-silent-man type smile and squeezed Mary's hand.

'I didn't notice you when I came in,' Mary said to Barney.

'I saw you come in, but I didn't recognize you at first glance,' he replied. 'You look different.' One eyebrow went up a fraction. 'You look good.'

'It's amazing what make-up'll do.'

'There's more to it than that, honey.'

Flattered, Mary relaxed a little. 'What're you doing with yourself these days?'

'Playing the field,' Barney said smoothly, his top teeth protruding as he smiled. 'How about yourself? I notice you're not with Betty.'

'No. I'm sort of soloing, now.'

Barney looked interested. He was about to say something when Derek asked him where the Gents was. Barney told him, and when Derek had gone he leaned close to Mary. 'Look, I couldn't say this before, not while I was going around with Betty – but I've always fancied you a bit. More than a bit.' His face had gone stiff with sincerity. 'I wanted you to know that, Mary.'

'Oh. Well . . .' Mary lowered her eyes winsomely. Her mind was racing. 'It's funny, that . . .'

'What do you mean?'

'I – well, it's not easy for me to say . . .' She looked at

Barney for an instant, then lowered her eyes again. 'All the time Betty was going with you, I tried not to admit it to myself, but I quite fancied you, too.'

Barney stared at her. 'And now, when we're both on our own, as you might say, we bump into each other. Amazing.'

'Yeah,' Mary said, 'it really is, isn't it?'

'Miraculous. Makes you believe in fate, eh?'

Mary was sure that whatever Barney was thinking, she was well ahead of him. This was a stroke of luck that proved something to her: if she wanted something badly enough, and made a real effort, she could get it.

'Listen.' Barney's voice was low, verging on husky. 'We're going on to a party. Derek and me, that is. Want to come?'

The ploy flashed into Mary's head an instant before she put it into action. 'I've got to be in early,' she said. 'But what if you send Derek on to the party and tell him you'll see him there later on?'

Barney frowned, then his face cleared and he smiled. 'We could maybe pop round to my place for a little while – just to celebrate our new understanding, know what I mean?'

Mary nodded. 'That's what I was thinking we could do.'

'Great idea, Mary.' Under the table, Barney's hand spidered along her thigh and gave it a squeeze.

Better than a great idea, Mary thought. A *brilliant* idea. There would be time to celebrate in whatever way Barney wanted, and time to talk a little; she could delicately bring up the matter of her need for cash – she would say it was for Christmas presents, just to put herself in the best light. And she would be home on time. Home with the price of the gig and probably more –

home, she promised herself, with a solid deal made, one that would guarantee her a regular income.

She smiled brightly at Derek as he came back to the table. Simultaneously she stroked Barney's hand, realizing that she was a lot sharper than people knew. Or than she'd known, before tonight.

6

There were fewer than fifty people in the room. Betty Crookes had expected more, but she was glad there weren't.

'If you want a drink, chuck, just help yourself.' Gilbert, Giro Ripoff's chief roadie, pointed to a trestle table along one wall. 'I think there's just about everything you'll want there.' He gave Betty's backside a firm pat and moved on to deliver the same message to a pair of girls who had just come in.

Betty could scarcely believe this had happened. There she'd been, still reeling from the impact of the concert, shuffling towards the exit among hundreds of other fans, when Gilbert edged his way through the crowd and thrust a card into her hand. It said

THE BAND WOULD LIKE YOU TO COME TO THE PARTY.
HANG ON TO THIS CARD.

The address of a hotel was printed at the bottom. Betty pocketed the card. When she was outside she told her mates to go back to the station without her, she would be getting a lift. She found the hotel, showed her card to a weary-looking man at reception, and was told to go to Conference Suite C. And here she was. There was no sign of the band, but there was a lively, expectant atmosphere in the room. A tall hi-fi unit played Giro Ripoff's album, friendly roadies circulated and girls giggled and chattered nervously, most of them sounding as surprised to be there as Betty was.

The lighting was very low. As Betty crossed to the drinks table she peered into a dark space between the hi-fi unit and a curtained window. Someone was standing there, a girl, keeping herself out of sight as she gulped her drink. She turned as Betty approached.

'Oh, hello.'

Betty peered closer, trying to see who it was.

'You got invited too, did you?' Mary stepped out of the shadows, smiling awkwardly.

'Oh, it's you, kid.' Betty made an awkward smile of her own. 'Well, well.'

They stood examining each other, Betty in her fun-fur jacket, black mini and mesh tights, Mary in new diamond studded leathers, her hair back-combed into a blue-streaked nimbus.

'You're looking pretty good,' Betty said. 'The make-up's tricky.'

Mary nodded, acknowledging she had done a neat job. The pale foundation and light pink lipstick dramatized the effect of dark-rimmed eyes, exaggerated eyebrows and purple-shaded eyelids.

'Looks like it paid off,' she murmured.

'What – the make-up?'

'No. Us hanging near the band the way we've done. We've got accepted.' Mary looked around at the other girls. Some were with boys, but the majority were unescorted. 'Do you reckon these are all groupies?'

Betty shrugged. 'Don't know. I doubt it, though. I reckon most of them are here for the first time. Like us.'

'Maybe that's how it works. You get invited to one party and that's that.'

'God, I hope not.' To be a groupie, a girl had to do

65

more than follow a band from gig to gig. She had to become part of the unit, doing little jobs for the lads, fetching and carrying – and, of course, sleeping with them. 'Now I've got my foot in the door,' Betty said, 'I'm wedging my way right in.'

'Me too.'

Betty picked up a drink, not bothering to check what it was, since she drank anything. 'Mary . . .'

'Yeah?'

'Are we mates again?'

'Sure we are.'

They smiled at each other, though Mary couldn't keep her eyes on Betty's for more than a second.

'How did you manage to make it to the concert, anyway?'

'I came into some money,' Mary said. 'The usual way.'

Betty nodded, impressed. 'How about your folks? How come they let you out?'

'They didn't. I took off this morning. Told them I'd be back at the usual time.'

'Christ, they'll have the law out hunting for you.'

'No, they won't,' Mary said. 'I left a note with our Brendan and told him to give it to Mum at teatime.' It had taken Mary a long time to write the note. She hoped her mother would be able to read it.

'They'll go mad, Mary. You know what your old lady's like.'

'Yeah, I know.' Mary looked around the room and gave a little shiver. 'I don't care. Anything was worth that concert. And now there's this. I don't care what anybody does. This is worth *anything*.'

The door opened sharply and everyone stopped talking. They stared as Sam, the band's leader, stood in the opening and stared back. He was tall, with long bleached hair and a shaggily sculpted beard. His expression, hard-eyed, almost glowering, suggested he was going to throw everybody out.

'God, he's gorgeous,' Betty breathed.

A sudden smile cracked Sam's face. 'Hi,' he said. As he stepped into the room the other three appeared behind him, theatrically timing their saunter as they flanked Sam towards the drinks table.

The gathering became animated. The music was turned up and girls made excuses to cluster near the musicians. Roadies encouraged other girls to dance with them. Mary and Betty remained where they were, a few feet from the spot where Sam and the squat little drummer, Mike, were helping themselves to large whiskies. The other two, Chris and Dave, had been surrounded by five girls. One of them was hanging on to Dave's arm and cuddling up to his shoulder. Two girls were talking to Chris at the same time.

'Do you think they'll say anything to us?' Mary asked.

'Sooner or later, kid.' Betty's eyes were glued on Sam as he poured whisky down his throat.

'Come on girls,' Gilbert said, appearing beside them with fresh bottles for the drinks table. 'Mustn't be wall-flowers, eh? Get out on the floor and shift your buns a bit.'

Betty swallowed some of her drink and winked at Mary. 'Might as well enjoy ourselves while we're here.' She banged the glass down on the table, attracting Sam's attention long enough to smile broadly at him.

Mary emptied her glass and joined Betty on the floor. The music wasn't designed to dance to, but there was a stomping sub-beat that was easy to move with. The girls stood side by side, making sharp rhythmic movements with their shoulders and shifting their feet. Everybody else was doing the same. The mass, uniform movement was hypnotic. Mary had never been much good in discos, but she found herself enjoying this.

As time passed the music got louder and a few of the girls discovered they were drunk. Joints began circulating. Mary detected the familiar, burning-leaves odour, hanging thick in the air. She wasn't good with joints. They made her dizzy and the day after she usually felt drained and depressed. But tonight she was going to do nothing to make herself appear un-cool. She wouldn't refuse a puff if she was offered. Instead, she would use a trick she'd learnt from another girl who didn't like hash. She would put the joint to her lips and blow down it gently. It looked just like inhaling, so long as she remembered to move her shoulders back as the end of the joint began to glow.

'Mind if I join in?'

Mary turned her head and saw little Mike, the drummer. He was standing close, his shoulder against hers as he fell in with the rhythm. Up close he had really bad acne.

'Enjoying yourself?' he asked.

'It's brill,' Mary assured him.

'It'll get better. This is just a warm-up.' Mike nodded towards the drinks table, which now had plates of food on it. 'Fancy taking a break for a snack?'

They pushed their way past the other dancers and forced a niche in the line of eaters and drinkers by the table. Mary had been craning her neck all the way across, trying to see where Chris was. But there was no sign of him. It was really big-time, being escorted like this by one of the band, but Chris was her dream. He was her idol. By comparison Mike was just a great drummer.

'These parties are always a bit square for starters,'

Mike said, loading a plate with Twiglets and cheese footballs. 'Even the grub's corny. But you have to keep up appearances. Until the night manager comes on, that is.' He explained that the booking of the suite was for a legitimate party, and the booking was handled by the senior manager of the hotel, who worked strictly by the book. But when the night manager came on duty, the sky was the limit. They moved to a penthouse suite. 'Not all of us, of course.' Mike winked at Mary. It hadn't anything like the effect of Chris's wink. 'We take maybe a dozen selected guests, if you get what I mean by *selected*.'

Mary had a rough idea.

'You'll be on the selected list,' Mike murmured, winking again. 'Have another drink, eh?'

In the course of the next ten minutes Mary learned a lot about Mike's view of himself. She discovered that he was into rebuilding himself. 'My earlier life dismantled me,' he explained. 'I had a lot of curiosity. I'm a born experimenter, right? But they wouldn't let me experiment with life. I had to conform. A real bummer. So I cracked. For a while I couldn't do any more than just exist. But after school I cut loose. I've been loose ever since, and I'm making myself the shape I want to be. I've got the freedom to do that now.'

Part of the process of rebuilding was the study and practice of total free expression. 'Whatever I fancy doing, I do it. Anything at all, even if it's something a bit, you know, taboo. Taboo even by our standards.' The wink again, then a more confidential tone of voice. 'To tell you the truth, you strike me as a girl who'd be a bit into experimenting.' Mike paused at that point, looking at Mary expectantly. She said it would all depend. Mike seemed to find that encouraging enough. 'How can we learn anything about ourselves if we don't touch every depth and follow every instinct? Answer me that.'

Mary didn't try. Mike didn't wait, anyway. He launched into an analysis of what was wrong with everybody in the world except, it seemed, himself. The way he described it, he was out ahead in the business of being a fulfilled human being. But he was still working on it. He wasn't going to get complacent.

Mary's chance to talk came when Mike asked her what kind of men she liked. She was well aware that he had earmarked her for his own, as far as that evening was concerned, but even so she had to tell the truth whether it hurt Mike or not. She felt it would be bad luck to lie about something like that.

'I like men like Chris,' she said.

'What – *our* Chris?'

'Yeah.'

Mike looked astonished.

'Except that I don't know any other guys quite like him,' Mary went on. 'Not any that are even a little bit like him, as it happens.' She was going to leave it there, but two drinks and half of a third had made her tongue more supple than usual. 'To tell you the absolute truth, men have never done much for me, until I saw him. He's like – well, like a god to me.'

Mike shook his head. 'Don't get me wrong, love,' he said, tight-lipped, 'but you'd *better* be somebody that likes experimenting, if you want to tangle with Chris.'

Conversation between them more or less died at that point. After a few more idle observations Mike wandered away, leaving Mary alone at the corner table, feeling light-headed from the drink and the cannabis fumes. She still couldn't locate Chris and now there was no sign of

70

Betty, either. She decided to go back to the middle of the room and join the dancers again.

At around two in the morning things began to change. The roadies, rather less friendly now, began herding people out of the suite in groups. Mary had been leaning on the wall, talking to another girl about the band and how much it had changed both their lives, when she noticed the cleaning-up operations begin. The music got quieter. Extractors above the windows hummed, clearing the air. Then the music stopped. The band seemed to have gone. Mary felt a tight pang of disappointment. They were going to tell her to go home. She should have been nicer to Mike, she realized. It had been a bad move, a crazy move, telling him how she felt about Chris. How would she ever get close to Chris now?

A roadie came across. He was a big pear-shaped lad in jeans and a striped tee-shirt. 'Time to go home now, love,' he said. Mary swallowed hard, trying to muster some kind of appeal. Then she realized he was talking to the girl beside her. He hadn't even looked at Mary. He waited until the girl had gathered up her bag and coat and then he saw her to the door, where some others were being ushered out.

Mary looked round the room. There were about ten other girls and herself. Some of them obviously knew each other; others, like Mary, stood alone, looking half happy, half apprehensive. Mary stayed where she was, waiting and hoping.

After a few more minutes, as hotel staff began stacking chairs, casting cold looks at the girls as they worked, the big roadie came across again. 'Get in the lift and press the top button,' he told Mary. 'When you get out, it's the door right in front of you. Just go straight in.'

Trembling, Mary did as he said. She found herself

outside a dark-blue lacquered door with a big spherical silver knob. She wiped her sweating palms on her jacket, reached out and turned the handle. As she stepped inside, walking on carpet that sighed under her feet, she saw Chris at once. He was standing at the far end of the hall. He was with Mike and Sam. Between Mary and the three band members there were four or five girls, hanging up jackets, flouncing their hair and talking nervously. Mary hardly saw the other girls. All she could see was Chris. And he was looking at her.

Mike broke away and approached her. 'Come on, kiddo,' he said dryly, scratching his boxer's nose. 'I'll introduce you to your idol.'

Mary followed him along the hall, almost stumbling with nervousness. Chris was still looking at her, his eyes dreamy, curious. Mary gulped softly and hoped she would be able to speak.

Reg Smith was by the living room window, arms folded, jaw stiff. It was raining and he had been watching the runnels on the glass for five minutes. It was a boring thing to do, but it was better than looking at his wife, who hadn't opened her mouth since he came in from the pub. She was in her chair by the fireside, her scrawny frame hunched forward, her face a motionless study in disapproval. Her angle and expression were a code Reg could read at a glance. Theresa was telling him that, on top of her outrage over Mary's behaviour, she now felt very annoyed at him for going out for his Sunday lunch-time pint, as if nothing had happened.

'Twenty-past two,' Theresa finally snapped.

'I know what time it is,' Reg grunted.

'So where is she?'

'You know what the trains are like on a Sunday. Few and dead slow.'

'And where was she all last night?'

'My crystal ball's on the blink,' Reg snapped. 'And don't start going over all that again. I've had it off you since I got up. I don't need a repeat.'

Theresa groaned, a sound like an old door moving on clogged hinges. 'I don't understand you. She's a fifteen-year-old girl. A minor. And she's run off to some heathen pop concert, even though we told her she couldn't go, and she's stopped out *all night*. It's disgraceful, Reg. Disgraceful. And yet you behave as if nothing's wrong.'

'I'm as worried and upset as you are,' Reg said, still facing the window. 'I'm just not making such a noise about it, that's all.'

'Lord knows what Percy and Ida thought.'

'It doesn't matter a damn what they thought.' Reg turned. 'They got a chance to show off their snooty affront, didn't they? I should think they're content enough with that.'

'She knew they wanted to see her. She knew. Yet she – '

Theresa, for God's sake! I don't want to hear any more about it!'

Theresa thrust herself out of her chair. She held up a trembling finger under Reg's nose. 'I don't care what you say, I'm going to speak to Father Burke about her. If you can't control her, maybe he can.'

'It's none of that bloody priest's business!'

'Don't swear about him!'

Reg was colouring. 'Swear about him? I'll swear *at* him if he sticks his beak into this. Religion's gotten to be a disease with you, Theresa. A person's only got to fart out of place around here and you've got the priest in.'

73

'You can't open your mouth without filth pouring out!'

'Aw, bloody hell.' Reg turned away, heading for the kitchen. 'I'll shut myself away from you, in case you get infested with my devils, eh? That's what they call it when you take the risk of living with an unclean spirit in the house, isn't it?' He stood in the kitchen doorway for a moment, glaring at Theresa, then he slammed the door shut.

Out on the street Mary heard the door bang. She paused and looked up, wondering vaguely what it was, then carried on walking. She felt as if she had been on her feet all day. She'd had to walk from the hotel to the station because it was raining and there were no taxis; at the station she had to stand in the buffet because all the seats were taken, then after an endless wait, she had to stand on the train, too.

Back in Stockport she walked to Barney's place and let herself in with the key he'd given her. He was away on a weekend job so Mary had the place to herself; she was pleased about that, because she didn't think she could face anybody like Barney today. She got out of her leathers, washed and changed into her jeans and sweater. When she'd brushed the colour out of her hair and changed the style back to a dowdy one, she put away her gig clothes – Barney had already told her she could keep her gear at his place – and set off to walk home.

At her front door she fumbled out her key and stood looking at it for a moment. She had deliberately not thought about this moment, but now she was wondering how much flack she would catch. She wondered about it without worrying about it. The state of mind she was in, she was past caring what they would say or do.

Theresa was at the living room door before Mary had her first coat button undone.

74

'In here! This very minute!'

Mary hung up her coat and stepped in past her mother, not looking at her.

'Now. Explain yourself.'

The kitchen door opened. Mary saw her father come halfway into the room. He looked pretty mad. Mary folded her arms.

'I've been to a concert in Liverpool, like I told you in the note.'

'That's not good enough!' Theresa screeched.

Mary tightened her arms about herself and stared at the floor. They could say and do anything they wanted, she thought. She wouldn't be staying here much longer, anyway. She was leaving, first chance she got, and nobody would stop her.

7

On Christmas Day Reg Smith went to his local, the Malt Shovel, and had a midday drink with Jack Rivers, a man who worked for the same firm as Reg. They had been friends for more than ten years; they played on the same darts and crib teams, and on fishing trips they consulted each other on domestic, financial and most of their other personal problems. Although he was well aware that Christmas was hardly the time to bring up painful matters with a friend, Reg felt he had to talk to somebody, preferably another man with children the age of his own. Jack Rivers was the obvious choice.

'My oldest's turning out to be a right problem kid,' Reg said, as soon as he had the opportunity. He was sitting with Jack in a tiny booth at the end of the bar furthest from the door. Jack had a habit of mirroring people's expressions as they spoke to him; he frowned delicately as Reg's brows came closer together. 'For a while I thought she might be going through a phase, the way a lass does at her age. Head full of pop music, neglecting her school work, that kind of thing. But I'm not so sure it's a phase at all. It's the beginning of something, Jack. Something's happening to her, and it's not good, whatever it is.'

He explained about Mary defiantly going to the concert in Liverpool, and then staying away all night. 'And when we tackled her with it, she just dug her heels in. No proper explanation, no repentance. I don't feel I can get close to her any more. It's like there's a wall gone up between us. And because the wife and me don't see eye to eye on how to deal with Mary, it's put us at each other's throats. I can't remember a Christmas as miserable as we're having this year.'

'You were always close to young Mary,' Jack said, stroking his thinning hair. 'Like I was with Bill.' He thought for a moment. 'It's the same kind of story, really. He used to go everywhere with me. Football, swimming, even helped on the allotment. Then he started getting interested in motorbikes. He took less interest in doing things with me, and he started staying away from school, too. Then before we knew it he was into the motorbike cult, or whatever it is. Hanging round all the time with hairies in greasy leathers. Then that bloody awful business with drugs, and after that . . .' Jack shrugged. 'He moved out a year ago and I think I've seen him maybe three times since.'

It occurred to Reg that instead of managing to share a problem, he had inadvertently opened a wound. Jack had begun to look miserable.

'I'll tell you, Reg,' he said, 'it's all a mystery to me. I'm starting to see the change come over Sarah. She's just a bit younger than Mary. It's . . .' His fingers worried a beer mat as he tried to express what he felt. 'It's what you said, I suppose. There's a wall going up, brick by brick. The kids on one side, us on the other.' He sighed. 'It's at times like this, Christmas, that you feel it worst. There's a kind of feeling of loss.'

Reg remembered his feeling of loss in the town one day, watching Mary walk away from him. 'I'm worried about what's up ahead,' he murmured.

'Yeah.'

'If we knew what might happen, we could take steps, couldn't we? Try to prevent the worst of it. Head it off.'

Reg groaned softly. 'Christ, who knows what's going on in a kid's mind? And they're so sure they're right about things. Never a doubt, straight in with both feet.'

'It wasn't like this when we were kids,' Jack said, then flashed a little smile. 'Listen to me. Like one of them old buggers that sit beside the fire spitting pipe juice into the coals and complaining about everything.'

'But you're right. Things used to be different. We grew up to a pattern. Or most of us did. There was none of this rebellion or worshipping music and not giving a toss for anything else, not even your parents. God, when I think of it – me and my Dad were closer than sweat.'

Reg sat back, nursing his pint as he looked round the pub. Men sat in clusters at tables and on bench seats, most of them smartly dressed because it was Christmas Day. They looked happy enough, Reg thought, and yet a lot of them must be feeling as melancholy as he did. Christmas was a time for taking stock – or it certainly was as you got older. The stocktaking became more painful the older you got, too. There was a lot of heartache around, in spite of the smiles and the cheerful talk. And so much of the heartache was caused by children.

'This'll never do,' Jack said, slapping the table gently. 'We'll be crying in a minute if we keep it up.'

'True enough.' Reg gulped some beer and pointed to Jack's glass. 'Sup up. Maybe if we stun ourselves a bit we'll feel better.'

They drank two more pints each, accompanying them with talk of work, sport, past Christmases and a couple of jokes. As they left the pub, Jack turned to Reg and slapped his arm.

'Try to enjoy yourself today,' he said. 'I know you're worried about the lass, but it'll get you nowhere. Hope's all there is.'

'I suppose so.'

Waving, Jack made to turn away, then he stopped. 'There's one thing I reckon, Reg. It's no consolation, but it might be an explanation. About kids nowadays, I mean. They don't reach far enough. To get anything, you and me had to stretch, hadn't we? They don't have to now. There's so much handed them on a plate. They haven't developed the muscles for stretching, so all they bother with is what they can get at easily.'

It was an interesting notion and Reg thought it over as he walked home. It made sense, he decided. But it didn't make him feel any better. His heart still ached over Mary. Jack's explanation was all very well as far as it went, but it didn't give him peace, or even a clue about the truth of what was happening to his daughter. That was the trouble with explanations, he thought. They'd usually got nothing to do with the truth.

John Lennon had been murdered twelve days before the Liverpool concert. In the weeks that followed, Mary kept remembering how his death had overshadowed that party in the penthouse suite. Lennon's music wasn't anything like Giro Ripoff's; as far as they were concerned, that kind of stuff was a joke. But Lennon himself wasn't a joke.

Sam had said he'd known the ex-Beatle was going to be killed. Chris said he'd had a premonition about somebody in the pop business being murdered in New York. Mike and Dave both believed they sensed Lennon's presence, right there in the hotel. All four of them kept going back to the topic, throwing a cloud over the party, making it more like a wake.

Mary wondered if she would have enjoyed herself any more if John Lennon's ghost hadn't been there. She doubted it. In some ways she wished they had never invited her.

It had been Mike who spoiled everything, she was sure of that. Because of what she had said about Chris, about how she idolized him, Mike had got her up into that penthouse to humiliate her. When he introduced her to Chris, he had made it sound like she was with him. She never got to say another word to Chris after that. Mike had made sure she was too busy. All she could do was hear the talk, the terrible, depressing talk about John Lennon. And even then, she only heard them talking when she wasn't being mauled by the roadies. That had been the arrangement, engineered by spiteful little Mike. Mary had been laid on for the staff. Chris, Sam, Dave and Mike got it together with six or seven girls – between their bouts of gloomy death-talk – while Mary and two other females were passed around, as casually as the joints, among the roadies and other helpers.

In the morning she woke up lying in the apartment hallway, being told by a cleaner that she'd better clear out. Everyone else had gone. They had left her behind like some old cast-off. Like rubbish.

But that wasn't the way she told it to Betty.

On the Monday following the party Betty admitted she had been told to go home, along with most of the other girls, before the party moved upstairs. Her envy of Mary was open and a little raw. So Mary, to make herself feel better about what had happened, concocted a story about the great time she'd had with Chris.

'I've never had a night like it,' she concluded with feeling. 'Never, ever.'

It was more than a lie; it was a bout of wishful thinking, for Mary was sure that if Mike hadn't engineered matters, she *would* have had her opportunity to tell Chris how much she adored him – and she was just as sure he would have told her he felt strongly about her, too. That look on his face as she went into the penthouse had been like a clear, unspoken message. It was a message she wouldn't forget. In spite of what had happened, she was going to keep following the band until she got close to Chris. When she got close to him she would stay close.

Two weeks after Christmas something happened that bombshelled her plans to attend the band's next concert. She was coming out of a shop with some new clothes she'd bought when somebody rushed at her and knocked her against the shop window. The window rattled dangerously as Mary elbowed herself away from it. She looked up, regaining her balance, and a hand clamped her throat. She was pushed violently against the wall beside the shop doorway.

'I'll kill you, you bloody bitch!'

Mary gulped, trying to breathe, staring into little Betty's enraged face.

'Talk about a back stabber – you're lower than scum!'

Mary dropped her plastic shopper and grabbed Betty's wrist with both hands. She wrenched it aside and landed a slap on the side of Betty's head.

'Hoi, you two!' a policeman yelled from across the road. 'Pack it in!'

They both glared at him, then took a step back from each other. Mary picked up her bag and fussed with it until the constable had moved on.

'Cow!' Betty rasped. 'Been buying yourself some gear with his money, have you?'

'What're you on about?'

'You've been seeing Barney, haven't you?'

Mary read strong conviction on Betty's face, so she

decided not to deny anything. 'What if I have? You'd finished up with him, hadn't you?'

'That's got nothing to do with it.'

'He was free to make up his mind who he went around with.'

'Listen,' Betty said, her cheeks livid, 'you smarmed your way in there. Same way you oiled your way in with the band. And who carried you all the time, for months and months? Me. Muggins. I lent you money, stacks of it, and when I hadn't it to lend I helped you go out and earn it. You're a stinking cowing bitch and I'll get you for it.'

'When you're big enough you'll be too old,' Mary said, trying to sound unconcerned.

'I'll get you done, one way or another,' Betty insisted. 'Just for starters I'm going to blow up your little game with Barney.'

'And how do you plan on doing that, smart-arse?'

'I'll tell him everything. About you picking up men and doing it for money. About you spending his cash so you can go and have it off with a guy in a band. About you not even being sixteen yet – that and a lot more.'

'He'll never believe it,' Mary said, and walked away.

But Barney did believe it. When Mary showed up at his flat that night she could tell as soon as he answered the door. He was pale and slit-eyed. His lips were set in a tight line, only the very tips of his protruding teeth showing.

'Hi,' Mary said, trying to smile.

'Piss off.'

Now she tried to look puzzled.

'Don't come the innocent with me,' Barney said. His voice was throaty and unsteady. He pointed to a bag lying against the wall opposite the door. 'That's your stuff. Take it and shove off. Right now.'

'But what – '

There was a sudden bang in Mary's head. She hurtled sideways and her elbow cracked against the door jamb. Her ear sang as she spun away from the wall and staggered back. She realized Barney had hit her. He looked like he was going to do it again, but instead he turned, grabbed up the bag and threw it at her feet.

'Now *go*, before I really do batter you!'

She had a sore cheek, jaw and elbow for days, but the deepest pain came from the loss. From all the money Barney had given her she had saved nothing. Her mobility was gone and so was her major plan – to save every penny for a month and then take off.

She was devastated. Without cash she was imprisoned. Her pocket money was just a laugh, it didn't keep her a week in cups of coffee. There was nobody she could borrow from the next time there was a gig. It was terrible. It was disastrous. But she was still determined to break loose and be with the band.

On the third day of her dilemma she came home from school to find Father Burke waiting. His mouth was puckered tighter than usual, Mary noticed. Her mother's scowl was pretty severe, too – although it had been that way most of the time since the Liverpool concert.

'Hello, Father.' Mary felt extraordinarily calm. Depression had immunized her against most emotions, lately. She certainly didn't feel any anxiety about the priest being there.

'I'll get on with dinner,' Theresa mumbled, going to the kitchen.

Father Burke composed his hands in front of him,

folding them first one way, then another. He shook his head sadly. 'What's to be done with you, Mary Smith?'

Mary gave him a puzzled look.

'Don't pretend you don't know what I mean, my girl. I've had a long talk with your poor mother. She's worried to distraction about your behaviour. And I suspect she'd have kept it bottled up, if I hadn't called here today and made her talk to me. Have you any idea how much pain you've caused her?'

'I don't try to hurt anybody,' Mary said.

'You don't try to gladden anyone, either. You're too wrapped up in yourself, too selfish. The one person you're going to hurt most, in the end, is Mary Smith. You'll wither your immortal soul with your behaviour.'

Mary shrugged impatiently. She had never been able to swallow religion and now she didn't even feel like concealing her indifference. She noticed Father Burke had stiffened indignantly.

'Don't you care that you're in mortal danger, girl?'

'I suppose not.' Mary surprised herself. She hadn't thought she was going to say that out loud.

'You wicked girl!' Burke unclasped his hands and for a moment Mary thought he was going to hit her. 'Get on your knees, *now*, and beg God's forgiveness!'

Now Mary did feel something. It was resentment, with a touch of anger. She frowned at the priest. His face was churning, radiating his displeasure.

'On your knees, girl!'

'No.'

The kitchen door flew open. Theresa stood there, glaring. 'Mary! Do as the Father tells you!'

'I won't.' In her head Mary felt icy coldness, a determination to resist that she'd never known before. She looked at the priest, then at her mother. 'You can't make me.'

Theresa rushed forward. 'I'll show you what I can do!' She caught Mary by the arm and tried to drag her in front of Father Burke. Mary twisted free.

'I'm not getting down on my knees for him or anybody else!'

Theresa glanced at Father Burke. He was doing his best to look outraged. 'Do you see, Father? I can't do a thing with her. Her father won't even try to. What am I going to do?'

'Leave the matter with me,' the priest said. He turned wrathful eyes on Mary. 'It is part of my duty, young woman, to rescue people, people like you, from their own wickedness. It's my duty and I will do my duty. You won't be allowed to continue with your wilfulness and your pursuit of sin. Do I make myself clear?'

'You're not my Dad,' Mary snapped.

'I'm your *priest!*'

Mary took in the tableau; her mother, frozen in an attitude of utmost shock, the priest beside her like a pink-faced avenging angel, and herself, the focus of their anger and dismay. It seemed empty, meaningless.

'I'm going to my bedroom.'

'You're staying right there and you're going to apologize to Father Burke!'

Mary picked up her school bag, turned and walked through to her room. She went in and closed the door. She stood still for a minute. When she was sure her mother wasn't going to come in she went and sat on the bed.

'That's that, then,' she murmured, looking at a photograph of Chris. She wasn't going to stay there any longer. She still had no idea how she would get out. But it was what she had to do.

8

'If I'd known I was going to last this long,' Sergeant Lowry said, 'I'd have taken better care of myself.' He patted his round stomach three times and belched softly. 'The doctor tells me I'll only ever enjoy my retirement if I get myself on a diet and stick to it. Now I ask you, Willis, how in hell can I get any pleasure out of my retirement if I can't eat the grub I like? Eating's one of my hobbies.' He paused, frowned at the dashboard, then corrected himself. 'It's my only hobby.'

Constable Willis smiled. He liked being on duty with the sergeant. He was never bossy and never pulled rank. Being out on the job with Sergeant Lowry was like having a day off.

'How long have we got to wait for this lot, Sarge? You talking about food's making my belly rumble.'

'We'll give them another five minutes with the child welfare geezer, then I'll nip in and explain we've got to get back to base. Here . . .' Willis fumbled in a pocket of his uniform jacket and produced a crumpled paper bag. 'Have a humbug. It'll keep the pangs at bay.'

They had been sitting in the squad car outside Bradford's central police station for twenty minutes. Sergeant Lowry had already been inside to identify himself and verify the identity of the two young people he had come to escort back to Stockport.

'These kiddie-welfare types like to deliver lectures,' Constable Willis said. 'I sometimes think they do more harm than good. A kid needs discipline and guidance, not a lot of do-gooding hot air.'

'Don't be too hard on them. They've got a rotten job. It'd send me up the wall if I'd to see half the cases they deal with.'

Willis took the point with a nod. He had been in the force for three years and driving town-centre patrols for half of that time. Cases involving young people had given him some of his sadder and nastier memories. There was nothing especially sad or unpleasant about today's job, though. Two teenage kids had run away and were being taken back home. It was routine, just minor tearaway stuff.

'Looks like we're on a bonus, Sarge.' Willis pointed to the side door of the station. A man with flyaway grey hair was leading a boy and girl down the steps.

'Right. Get the back open, son.' Sergeant Lowry opened his door. 'I'll say ta-ta to the welfare bloke.'

The boy, lanky and dour-faced, was glaring aggressively at Lowry as he approached. The girl was expressionless, her eyes fixed on the ground as she shuffled forward.

'It's home-time then, kids.' The sergeant smiled at the welfare officer. 'Two more off your hands, eh?'

'We've enough without the migrating variety,' the man said, returning the smile. He followed as Lowry led the pair to the car and ushered them into the back seat.

When the door was shut the sergeant turned and jerked his thumb at his passengers. 'What do you reckon? One-off jobs, or are they habitual types?'

'The boy's pretty scared, I think, even though he's keeping up the hard front. I'd imagine this experience has put enough wind up him to keep him on the rails, as long as he's supervised a bit more closely in future. I'm not so sure about the girl, though.'

'Hard case?'

'No. She's stubborn, though. As good as told us she'd run away again, first chance she gets. I fancy she might, too. And there's not going to be a lot anybody can do about it. Not if she's determined.'

'Kids,' Lowry sighed. 'Thanks for all your trouble, anyway.'

'It's what we're here for.'

The men shook hands briefly and Sergeant Lowry got into the car. 'Home, James,' he murmured, 'and don't spare the horsepower.'

They had been driving for five minutes before the sergeant decided to break the wall of silence between himself and the pair in the back. He turned and smiled at them.

'Feel better now you're going back home? All that living rough couldn't have been much fun.' There was no response. The boy stared straight ahead. The girl gazed at her clasped hands. 'What do you say, Mary?' the sergeant urged her. 'Surely it's better to be at home getting looked after properly, eh?'

Mary shrugged.

'Especially this time of year,' Lowry said. 'January's the coldest month, I reckon. A person could perish out in this weather. Even young, strong persons like you two.' He produced his bag of sweets and offered it to them. 'Here, have a humbug.'

'No ta,' the boy said sharply.

'Mary?'

'I don't like humbugs, thanks.'

'Suit yourself.' Lowry offered the bag to Constable Willis, who nodded and popped a sweet into his mouth. Lowry took two and sat back, savouring the flavour as he rolled the toffees around his tongue. After a minute he turned again and looked at the boy. 'What made you want to run away anyway, Peter? I'm curious about things like that. I never wanted to run away when I was your age. They'd a job to get me to leave home at all, actually.'

Peter sniffed.

'Isn't it nice at home, or what? I was round there last night, just after we'd got word that the Bradford police had found you. It seems a very nice home you've got, son. And you've a grand mum and dad, too. They were dead worried about you. Didn't it occur to you that they'd be upset?'

Peter sniffed again, but this time he looked at the sergeant. 'Not everything's what it seems,' he said, barely moving his lips.

'What do you mean?'

'Just what I say. Work it out for yourself.'

Constable Willis looked sharply at the mirror. There were times when he believed the sergeant took too much lip from young people.

'Are you telling me your home isn't really a nice place – and your folks aren't nice people?'

'Yeah, that's what I'm telling you. Our house is a square's paradise and the two squares that run it want everything and everybody else in it to be the same. Square.'

'But you're not square?'

'I know where some things are at,' Peter snapped.

'My son used that expression,' Lowry said. '"Where it's at." That expression.'

'Maybe he's a switched-on guy,' Peter said.

Lowry shook his head, his expression staying friendly. 'He was about sixteen when he used the expression. Used it a lot. He's thirty, now. It must be quite an old-fashioned expression by now. So's "square", when you think about it.' Lowry smiled, slow and easy. 'Maybe if you spent less time getting an image of yourself, son, you'd be able to see things around you in a clearer light. You've put labels on your home and parents – now doing that really *is* square. No place or person is absolutely anything. Try seeing the virtues and advantages of living where you do. And have a go at seeing your parents' point of view now and again.'

Peter was staring ahead again, his jaw grinding irritably. Lowry switched his attention to Mary. 'How about you, love? Fed up with where you live? Having a hard time with your folks?'

'With my Mum,' Mary said.

'I saw her last night, too. She seemed pretty worried, just like Peter's mother.'

Mary twined her fingers tightly and stared at them.

'Your dad wasn't at home when I called, but he came round the station later on. If you ask me, the man's been heartbroken. He said he's hardly slept since you did your vanishing act – what was it, nine days ago? Something like that. He's been looking for you. Everywhere he could think of.' Lowry shifted in his seat, bringing himself closer to Peter and Mary. 'What made the pair of you run away to Bradford, of all places?' He already knew the answer, but he wanted to hear them try to rationalize what they had done. 'It doesn't have a very exciting ring to it, running off to Bradford. London I can just about understand, but Bradford? How come?'

'The band,' Mary said. 'I wanted to go to the concert.'

'What band's that?'

'Giro Ripoff.'

'Are they good?'

'They're the best.' Mary's voice carried some life now.

90

'What about you, Peter? Did you go to see the band too?'

Peter nodded.

'Why didn't you come back after the concert, then?'

'I was . . .' Peter stopped himself and glanced at Mary. She glanced back, then looked at Sergeant Lowry.

'Was it your idea to stay on in Bradford?' Lowry asked her.

She nodded. 'I wasn't going back, anyway. I'd made my mind up about that. I met Peter after the concert, recognized him from back home. We got talking. He decided he wanted to stay away too.'

'You pooled your cash, was that it?'

'That's right,' Mary said.

'But it didn't last and you tried to get into a hostel. And that's when the police were told about you.' Lowry sighed. 'What did you think you could do? Didn't you realize you'd have to go back home, sooner or later?'

'We could have got jobs,' Mary said. 'With the band.'

'Doing what? Fetching and carrying, that kind of thing?'

'Yeah. I've met some of them in the band. I know them, they'd have given us something to do. But they changed the date of the second Bradford gig. They took off the same night as the concert we went to. We were waiting for them to come back.' Mary turned her head and gazed balefully out of the window. 'They'll be back the day after tomorrow.'

'Well, I don't know anything about this band,' Lowry said, 'but I'd say you were lining yourself up for a whole lot of misery, tagging on to them. You must have heard plenty of stories about lads and lasses that get mixed up with pop bands. They'd have been breaking the law, for starters, if they'd given you jobs. It wouldn't have led to

91

anything but trouble – bad trouble.' Lowry paused, looking at Mary. 'What happens now? Are you going to settle down a bit and let this phase blow over? Take my word for it, love – it *is* only a phase.'

'I don't want to stay at home,' Mary said.

Lowry watched her in silence for a minute, taking in her spiky nervousness, her restless eyes. 'Are you prepared to break your father's heart, love? Are you that determined?'

'I don't want to break anybody's heart.'

Later that day Mary's own words came back to her. She was sitting at a table in a bare little room at the police station in Stockport. Her father sat opposite. He looked as if his heart had truly been broken. He was bleary-eyed and sad-mouthed. His hair was tousled and he was unshaven. He had been up half the night arguing with her mother, he told Mary, and for the rest of the time he had been catching up on work he had let slip in the days she had been missing from home. In the few minutes they had been talking, Reg had offered Mary no rebuke. All he had done was say how much he had missed her, and worried for her.

'Promise me you'll not do this ever again,' he said now. 'I know you don't exactly get on with your mother, but she's been frantic. She loves you as much as I do, Mary.'

'What was she arguing with you about? Wanted to get me made a ward of court, did she? I've heard about that, it's happened to some girls at my school.'

'We were arguing about, oh . . .' Reg shook his head. 'Mostly it was about our different ways of looking at things. Your mother still thinks the priest should get more of a hand in dealing with you, I say he shouldn't.

She says you want hard discipline, I say you maybe need more understanding. We – '

'Dad,' Mary interrupted. 'I'll never get on with Mum. That's why I can't promise you I'll not leave again. I just want you to know I'm not doing it to hurt you. I'd do anything not to hurt you.'

'Then stay with us, Mary.'

'It would never work out – '

'Mary!' Anger flared for a second, widening Reg's eyes, making him grip the edge of the table. 'I can *make* you stay at home!'

'Nobody'll do that,' Mary said quietly. 'One way or another, I'd always be wanting to get away.'

Reg put his head down into his cupped hands and groaned. 'God, if I could only get you to understand . . .'

And would *he* ever understand? Mary wondered. Did her poor long-suffering father understand what it was like to be fired by an obsession, to be caught by a drive so powerful that every other consideration had to take second place? She had been away from home for well over a week, and rough as it had been she knew she would choose that kind of hardship, every time, sooner than the suffocating imprisonment her family wanted to go on imposing on her.

'What's to happen to me now?' she asked.

Reg lifted his head and looked at her. 'I'm taking you home. That's all. I've finished with all the formalities here. We can go whenever you feel up to it.'

'I thought Mum would have made some kind of trouble for me with the police.'

'About the money, you mean?'

Mary nodded.

'No, there'll be no trouble about that.' Reg looked at the table. 'That hurt me, Mary. Your mother, too. It could have caused a lot of problems, but I managed to square things. I had a bit saved.'

'I'm sorry.'

'It's all right.' Reg looked up. 'Really it is.'

There had been over fifty pounds. Theresa kept it in a jar on a high shelf in a kitchen cupboard. It was added to each week for a month, then banked, and then the bundle began to grow all over again as neighbours gave Theresa the instalment money for goods they bought from her catalogue.

'Let's get back, then,' Reg said, standing.

Mary got up. 'Is Mum going to go on at me?'

'No, love, I don't think so.'

When they got to the house there was no sign of Theresa. Brendan and Gary were there, building a Lego battleship on the dining table. They seemed shy of Mary.

'Where's your mum?' Reg asked.

'Church,' Brendan grunted.

'Church?'

'Mm. Said she was going down to see Father Burke.' Brendan glanced at Mary then added, 'She was crying a bit, then when she stopped she put on her coat and said she was going to see the Father.'

Mary looked at Reg. 'I hope she's not bringing that one back here,' she said. 'I won't let him talk to me, Dad. I don't have to.'

'Just put your things in your room,' Reg said, 'and don't fret about anything. I'll get the kettle on.'

In the bedroom Mary put down her bag and stared at the walls. Her posters, the few she had left behind, were gone. In their place were three holy pictures and a text, done in a florid script:

I ABHOR MYSELF
AND REPENT
IN DUST AND ASHES.

Mary didn't understand it, but she felt its unpleasantness. Having that thing nailed up over her bed was like having her mother's living presence in the room, glowering and full of reproach.

She looked at the other things – the dressing table she'd had since she was ten, the chest of drawers, the bedside cabinet and the oval rug. Mary felt no attachment to any of them. They gave off no warmth. As the seconds ticked past she began to sense the tightness of the house around her, the awful feeling of being gripped by it and doubled over by its weight.

Out beyond the living room she heard the front door open and close. A moment later she heard her mother's voice, a low, undulating whine. Her father spoke then, with a note of warning. There was a flurry of muted speech as they both spoke at once, then there was silence, as tangible as black cloth. Mary took a long deep breath and walked through to the living room. The boys were watching her and their mother furtively, pretending to carry on with the building of their battleship.

Theresa was by the fireside, warming her hands, pretending not to see Mary. Reg was at the kitchen door, waiting to intervene if he had to.

Theresa finally turned from the fire. 'So you're back, then,' she muttered, appearing to address the empty armchair beside Mary.

'Yes,' Mary said. 'But I didn't want to come back.'

Theresa glared at her with wide, stinging eyes. Her mouth opened in an oval, the shape of a raging howl. What escaped was a guttural hiss. She clamped her eyes shut and began to shake as the anger and hurt jerked her head from side to side.

Turning, Mary looked at Reg and said, 'I don't want any tea, thanks. I'll be in my room if you want me.'

Reg watched her go and listened as her bedroom door closed. It was a sharp, final sound, reminding him of something snapping loose and being lost.

'Sit down, Theresa. I'll bring you a cup of tea.' Reg looked at the boys, bowed over their work now, fingers busy, ears alert. 'Take that stuff through to your room, lads.'

They sullenly obeyed, pulling the structure apart into chunks they could easily carry. Reg watched Theresa sit down and bury her face in her hands. He went to the kitchen and set out two cups and saucers. As he poured the tea he began forcing himself to accept. He wasn't a man to take defeat lying down; he would resist whatever hurt was inevitably on its way, but underneath there would be a cushion of sorrowing acceptance. He could think of no other way to withstand the time ahead.

9

Between mid-February and the end of July, 1981, Mary ran away from home three times. On the first occasion the police picked her up in north Wales, trying to thumb a lift near a motorway slip road. She was taken back to Stockport, where she was put on a social worker's visiting list and warned, at weekly intervals, about the moral and physical dangers lying in wait for a girl who takes it into her head to cut loose from family and home. The second time she went away it was Reg who brought her back. He saw an advertisement for a Giro Ripoff concert in Leeds and turned up at the venue as the crowd was coming out. Mary had been easy to spot, though rather less easy to catch when she saw her father coming at her through the sardine-jam of bodies. When he finally had a grip on her and managed to persuade her there was no point in struggling or protesting, she got in the car with him and allowed herself to be taken home. Between that time and the day in July when she ran away for good, Mary became thoroughly sullen and uncommunicative. On the afternoon of her last day at St Bridget's, a teacher remarked to a colleague that the girl had a disturbing, feral quality.

'What does feral mean?'

'Something domesticated that's gone wild.'

'She never struck me as particularly wild.'

'It's under the surface. Like with some insane people, the kind that are able to appear normal, until you look really close and see the madness behind their eyes.'

'Feral' was not one of the words on Mary's final school report. Other words – 'inattentive', 'slow', 'vague', and even 'obtuse' – were used to summarize eleven years of failed attempts, by numerous people, to instil the rudiments of education in a girl who would have no commerce with reading, writing, arithmetic or religion. Mary threw the report in a waste bin on her way home. The same night she took a change of clothes and a sponge bag full of make-up to the Ladies near the centre of town, Transformed from a sixteen-year-old to a woman apparently three or four years older, she picked up three men in the space of two hours and returned home with forty-five pounds and an indelible mistrust of fatherly types in tidy suits. The following morning, early, she packed as many clothes as one holdall would carry and left the house so stealthily she didn't even disturb the cat.

The band were doing a one-night concert in Stoke-on-Trent. After being told at the theatre that the performance was sold out, Mary managed to buy a ticket in a nearby café, from a girl who was tempted to part with it for double the price she had paid.

The show produced a spiritual impact on Mary equivalent to that felt by her devout Irish grandmother, years before, on a visit to Lourdes. As the band crashed into their closing number Mary, in common with many people around her, felt a surge of sheerest ecstasy. She was cleansed. She was out and free, away from all authority and constraint. This time, she swore, no one would take her back to where she didn't want to be. Here was where she belonged, right at the heart of her adopted culture, the ambience of untethered spirits, the territory of liberated youth determined to let instinct have its head and impulse lead the way. At the final, air-rending crescendo from the band Mary screamed and went on screaming until there was no breath left in her.

Less than twenty minutes later she began to believe there was a lot to be said for blind faith. With no reasonable hope and purely from adoration, she was standing by the stage door, waiting for the band to come out. There was no van nowadays; the drill was that a big hire car would swoop up to the door, then two heavies would get out and make menacing gestures at the worshippers until the band were safely in the car and whisked away. Mary stood there with no sharp plan, no strategy to get herself near the boys. Her only scheme was to attend as many concerts as she could, to saturate herself with the nerve-message of the music and, somewhere along the way, worm herself into the band's retinue. Until that happy day, she believed she could keep herself fed and sheltered by abandoning every last qualm about doing whatever she had to for money.

But outside that theatre in Stoke-on-Trent the miraculous happened. A roadie came to the door, peering beyond the fans to see if the car was anywhere near. As the crowd surged closer he stepped back and suddenly his eyes fell on Mary. She stared back, remembering him. He was Gareth. He had been one of the men at the penthouse party in Liverpool. Mary gulped as he smiled at her. She wasn't mistaken, it was definitely her he was looking at – *beckoning to*.

Mary pushed her way through a cluster of other fans, some looking puzzled, others resentful.

'Hello again,' Gareth said, making an arch of his arm and beckoning Mary to pass under it. 'Just wait back there, huh?'

Mary didn't hesitate. She stepped into the passage behind the door. Three other girls were there. They

looked at her dully. Mary put down her holdall, said hi
and leaned on the wall, wondering.

Gareth pushed the door shut and came across. He took
Mary by the elbow and led her a few yards apart from
the others. 'You got a couple of hours?' he murmured.

'Sure.'

'Fine. Just hold on here.'

He walked away into the shadows of the corridor.
Mary leaned on the wall again and folded her arms.
There was a line in one of the band's numbers – *Don't
think, let it happen*. Mary ran it around in her head, *Dee-
DAH, Dee-Dee-DAH-DAH*, blanking thought, holding
off anticipation. The other girls were glaring at her. She
smiled back. *Dee-DAH, Dee-Dee-DAH-DAH*.

'Things have changed a lot,' Gareth said. 'Everything's
more organized now. Smoother. The band sort of knows
where it is, where it stands. They've got a clear image of
themselves. Want another drink?'

Mary held up the moussec she had been sipping. 'I've
plenty of this one left, ta.'

'Hang on, I'll get one for myself. Got a thirst that'd
choke a horse.'

It was the poshest house Mary had ever been in.
Gareth had told her it belonged to Russell Bruce, the
man who was standing by the bay window talking to the
band. He was about thirty, dressed in the leather-and-
studs gear, but in an upmarket kind of way; it all looked
too new on him, too expensive. Even his spiked hair gave
the impression it had been done by a top hairdresser. He
was a businessman of some kind, really rich, and he was
a fan of Giro Ripoff. He had given them the run of the
house for the night, so that they could start out fresh in
the morning.

When Gareth came back with his drink Mary asked him who all the other people were. There were about twenty of them, apart from the band and their entourage.

'Friends of Russell Bruce,' Gareth said. 'They think it's trendy to mix with riff-raff like us.'

'Those other three girls, the ones that were waiting in the theatre – '

'Family,' Gareth said. 'They're with us. For the time being, anyway.'

'How did they get to be family?'

Gareth shrugged. 'It just happened. It always just happens. Nothing formal, you know? A chick tags along, and if she's not a nuisance or trouble of some kind and if we all get on with her – well, she's family.'

'I'd like to be family,' Mary said.

'No reason why you shouldn't be. As long as you're not trouble. I mean if there's somebody out looking for you or anything like that, the lads wouldn't want to know.'

'Nobody's looking for me.'

'Just drifting, are you?'

Mary nodded. 'I suppose you could say that.'

Gareth leaned forward, staring at her as if he was trying to see beyond the make-up. 'You're not under-age, are you? Not jailbait? The guys have got to be careful about that kind of thing.'

'I'm eighteen,' Mary said.

'Well, if the lads are agreeable – like I said, there's no formalities. If you're prepared to dig in and help and don't make waves, fair enough. But I'll warn you, we sometimes have to put up with some pretty rough digs. It isn't always fancy shacks like this. Nor hotels, neither. The accountant soon made the band pack in that lark.

101

They might be getting big, but they still have to watch the pennies.'

'I don't mind what kind of digs I'm in,' Mary said. 'And I'm a good worker.'

'Can you cook?'

'Of course I can.' It wasn't true, but she would have laid claim to tougher skills than cookery for a chance to get in with the band – for the opportunity to be near Chris. Mary glanced across the room at him. He was listening to something Russell Bruce was saying, his eyes narrowed, his mouth in a lopsided, sultry smile. Just seeing him made her feel shivery.

'I'll have a word with Mike,' Gareth said.

Mary frowned. 'About me being family, you mean?'

'Yeah. Mike's the only one that sometimes objects. He's funny about some girls. Little Zoe over there, he didn't like her at first, but Sam reckoned she was OK and Mike climbed down over that one. But he can get stubborn.'

Mary was pretty sure Mike didn't like her. She had seen him looking at her a couple of times, trying to remember who she was. It wouldn't be long before he remembered, if he hadn't already. He had engineered things in Liverpool so that she ended up with the road crew. That hadn't been an act of friendliness. It was spite. But it had happened only because Mary had said how much she liked Chris, so perhaps deep down Mike fancied her. Maybe she should play up to him, make him forget how he had felt in Liverpool. To do that she would have to unload Gareth, some way or another. There was no doubt he had invited her along because he fancied her – or, more accurately, because he remembered Liverpool and the kind of time he'd had with her there.

'You realize if you go along with us,' Gareth said,

'there'll be no money in it? I mean there might be the odd few quid now and again, but mainly what you get is your grub and a roof over your head in exchange for mucking in and keeping things, ah, friendly and that.'

'Fair enough,' Mary said.

'Just so long as you've no illusions, kid. Look, I'll go and have a word in Mike's ear right now, while he's at the drinks table. Don't go away.'

Mary tried to watch Mike's reaction as Gareth stood speaking close to his ear, but people kept breaking her line of vision. She was about to move closer when a woman touched her arm. Mary turned and looked at her. She was middle-aged and expensively dressed. She was half smiling, half frowning, examining Mary like some puzzling object that had just been unearthed.

'Pardon me asking,' she said, her voice hushed; 'but are you a groupie?'

Mary thought about her answer for a second. 'Well, I'm with the band.'

'You go round with them everywhere, do you?'

Mary nodded, enjoying the sensation of fantasy being transformed to reality. 'Everywhere they go.'

'You do forgive me asking, don't you? It's all so new to me – I mean in the flesh, if you follow. I've read about groups and groupies and so forth, and I've seen pictures as everyone else has, but I've never had the opportunity actually to meet such people, until tonight.' Her voice dropped lower still as she said, 'It must be terribly exciting. Your life, I mean.'

'Yeah, it's not bad.' Mary glanced across at Mike. He was still listening to Gareth, rubbing his deformed nose, not looking too cheerful. She looked at the woman again. She didn't seem in a hurry to move away. 'What is it you do?'

'I'm in consultancy.'

Mary hadn't a clue what that meant, but she nodded anyway.

'Not an exciting life, of course. Not like yours. There are too many rules in my kind of existence. There's no space for free will.' Her eyes looked almost wistful. 'When I was younger I tried to kick over the traces. But I didn't kick hard enough. I was coaxed back into the fold. Nowadays, when I see a band like those young fellows over there, and I see girls like you – the last thing I want to do is condemn. To tell you the truth, the thing I feel most strongly is envy.'

Mary was touched. It was incredible that this woman, who looked and sounded like one of the wealthy aunts they had in television plays, should envy the likes of her. It was incredible and it was flattering. Mary hadn't often felt flattered.

'The life I lead is an endless chain of falsehoods, my dear. Lies to cover lies, lies in the service of lies – oh.' The woman stopped abruptly. 'Someone's trying to catch your attention.'

Mary turned and saw Gareth beckoning her across to the drinks table.

'It was lovely meeting you,' the woman said.

'Nice to meet you, too.' Mary said. As she went across to Gareth it struck her that that had been the only conversation she'd ever had with a woman of class. And she hadn't even been ticking Mary off.

'Mike wants to talk to you,' Gareth said. His expression didn't tell Mary whether Mike was in favour of her becoming family or not.

'What does he want to talk about?'

'No idea. He says for you to stick around near him for

a minute or two, until he can get away from the rest of them.'

'Did you ask him about me?'

'Yeah. He didn't say yes or no. Just said he'd like to talk to you.'

Mary loitered near the band for five minutes before Mike finally broke away and came over to her.

'Well then, Mary. How's tricks? Did you catch the show tonight?'

'Yeah. It was terrific. That drum solo of yours in the last number was amazing. Absolutely amazing.' Having just experienced the power of flattery herself, Mary was prepared to lay it on thick. 'I don't know how you do it, Mike.'

'It's one of those things,' Mike said, shrugging. 'Either you've got it or you haven't. A gift, right?'

'Yeah, I suppose so. A gift.'

'Listen, Mary . . .' Mike stepped closer. 'Big Gareth tells me you'd like to hang in with the band. Go on the road with us.'

'That's right. I'm a good worker, Mike, I really am. You'd not regret having me around.'

'I've no doubts about that, honey. But listen. It's not just anybody that can tag on to us. I mean where would we be if any old bit of tat could attach herself to the band, eh? Where would we be then, eh? Look, I've met you before and I reckon we'd get along all right. But before I say yes to you becoming one of the family, there's a favour I'd like doing.'

'What?'

'The gentleman by the window there, him in the classy leathers . . .'

'Russell Bruce.'

'Oh.' Mike looked impressed. 'You catch on fast. Got a good ear and you retain things. I like that, Mary.'

Now *he* was flattering her. Mary didn't find that very comfortable. On past experience it wasn't his style. 'What's the favour you want?'

'Ahem, well, Mr Bruce there, he's being pretty generous to us lot, letting us have the house, throwing in the booze and all the rest of it. Well the thing is, the other lads and me, we've caught on that he fancies getting friendly with one of the girls. He's done more than drop hints, if you get my drift. So I was wondering if you'd like to help us out.' Mike paused. 'It's not a favour I'd forget, Mary.'

Was it going to be *that* simple? Was Mike telling her that if she had a scene with Russell Bruce she was in, she'd be family? The one thing she wanted most in the world – or second most, because Chris was the ultimate dream, the big goal – was practically being handed to her, hassle-free. Unless Mike was putting one across her, of course. She could imagine him doing that, hitting out with the spite again, letting her think she was in, then giving her the boot as soon as the favour was attended to.

'What do you say, honey?'

'No problem at all, Mike. If I do it, will I be, you know, one of the crowd?'

'You've got my word on that.'

Mary looked him straight in the eye. He was levelling with her. Nowadays she could always detect when a man was telling her the truth. Or nearly always. It was one of the things she had learned the hard way.

'Just tell me what to do then,' she said.

'That'll be pretty much up to you – and Mr Bruce, of course.' Mike made an unpleasant snuffling sound which

Mary took to be a laugh. 'Come on, I'll introduce you to him.'

Mary moistened her lips and followed Mike. Dreams do come true, she told herself. You only have to work at them hard enough. She saw Russell Bruce turn and switch on his smile. It wasn't pleasant. He had the hooded look of some of the men she had been with, the ones she liked least of all. But this was still going to be a small price to pay.

'Russell,' Mike said expansively, 'this is Mary. She's been anxious to meet you.'

'Well, hello,' Bruce murmured. 'It's a pleasure, Mary.'

'Pleased to meet you.' From the corner of her eye Mary saw Chris, a yard away. He was looking at her. It hurt her to know that he knew what was going on here. She hoped it wouldn't spoil anything for her. That was something she could worry about later, though – right now there was a favour to be paid.

She made herself smile at Russell Bruce. The secret was to act everything out. As long as it wasn't real for her it would go over perfectly. The harder she acted, the more false it was, the easier they swallowed it. 'You've got a really beautiful house here, Russell.'

'And now I've got a guest to match it, eh?'

Mary watched the band melt away. She let Bruce put his arm round her shoulder.

'The nicest room in the place is for special guests only,' he purred at her ear. 'Why don't we have a drink and get to know each other, then I'll show it to you.' He made a leery grin. 'The room, I mean.'

'That'd be nice. Really nice.'

As they walked across to the drinks table the line began to drum again in Mary's head, a rhythmic chant that isolated her from all thought or foreboding. *Don't think, let it happen, Don't think, let it happen . . .*

107

10

The lingering pain inside Reg Smith – part of it sad resignation, the other part heartache – had changed by the time winter came. It had become worse than a pain, much worse than any grief he had ever known.

With Mary gone, he drew no consolation from what was left. Home, wife and children were no more than a steady reminder that the family was incomplete. Reg tried to be practical, though. He kept remembering that time is a healer, that it changes things; as the months passed, he told himself, the misery would change to something else. Whether it was time that had changed that pain inside him, he couldn't be sure. But it *had* changed. It had become a fear, the worst fear of all, the fear of dying.

He was as much puzzled as he was frightened. He had never before given serious thought to death. It was an event at a time in the dense mists ahead of him, no more to be considered than old age. But one day, parked in a lay-by, sitting in his cab warming his hands round a Thermos cup of coffee, Reg found himself wondering about how he would die, and when and where. The awful certainty that it would happen made cold sweat break on his face. Reg put down his cup and stared open-mouthed at the darkening sky.

It must happen.

How had he come to this? His long-burning hurt had transformed itself into terror. On the face of it, the terror seemed to have no connection with the loss of his daughter, yet instinctively Reg knew it had. For long minutes he sat there gazing at clouds layered on clouds, feeling his vulnerability and wondering what had made this dreadful change.

His coffee had turned cold before the answer came to him. It had been something his mate Jack Rivers had said almost a year ago, when they had gone to the Malt Shovel for a Christmas-Day drink. They had talked about Mary. Because that was the only serious conversation Reg had had about Mary with anyone outside of the family, it had stuck. Details of what Jack said had surfaced over the months, instead of being buried. One remark stood out clearer than the others, and had thrummed persistently at the back of Reg's mind: *I know you're worried about the lass, but it'll get you nowhere. Hope's all there is*.

Hope's all there is. Reg remembered something from childhood, a printed text like the ones Theresa liked to hang up all over the house. He believed it had been his mother's.

HOPE KEEPS LIFE'S
LAMP AGLOW.

Reg believed his hope had died. So what happened to life's lamp without hope? And was hope such a useful emotion anyway? Reg knew another saying, one his dad had often repeated: *He that lives by hope shall die of hunger*.

It wasn't so mysterious, this new terror, not when he thought about it clearly. His dearest hope, the shimmering dream he had carried since Mary was a toddler – it was gone, dashed to smithereens. It had been a hope that was probably stillborn, but it had sustained Reg for a long time. He had pictured his little girl growing to pretty womanhood, marrying well and giving him grandchildren. She was to have been the source of great happiness. So, now Reg could face the fact she was gone from him, he was left with nothing to contemplate but his own mortality. His hopes for Mary no longer stood between him and the fear of death.

Reg finally had to see a doctor. In the waiting room he rehearsed his story; he was jumpy all the time, depressed and unable to sleep, although he'd no idea why. That tale would surely get him some tranquilizers, something to take the edge off the paralysing fear that came at him regularly, without warning.

But Dr Raymond refused to settle for Reg's story. 'I'd like you to tell me more,' he said, putting his elbows on the desk and linking his fingers under his chin. He was a young man, smart and handsome, a prober with sharp eyes. 'What's going on in your mind when you're feeling jumpy, or when you're depressed? Is something worrying you?'

Reg looked at the steady eyes. He didn't see much chance of staying vague and getting away with it. But he decided to try.

'I'm just confused, mostly. Nothing special's worrying me, just the usual things – money, hanging on to my job, that kind of thing.'

'How's your relationship with your wife?'

'Fine.'

'Are you sure?' The doctor's head tilted a fraction. 'No tension between you, by any chance? Some unspoken resentment?'

'No. We get along fine.'

Dr Raymond winced faintly, as if he had felt a minor

110

twinge of pain. 'Mr Smith, your wife is a patient of mine. You're bound to know that.'

Reg nodded, feeling he had blundered into quicksand.

'Well, without breaching the confidentiality of the doctor-patient relationship, I have to say I find it remarkable that you say things are rosy between you.'

Reg tried to look blank.

'Imagine the picture as I see it,' the doctor said. 'Your wife's had medical difficulties that I don't have to go into, because you know all about them, I'm sure. Then there's been the emotional upheaval brought on by your daughter's recent behaviour. Faced with all that, your wife's in no state to get along fine, as you put it, with anybody.' Raymond's eyes closed for a second. When they opened they were harder, more incisive. 'Has your jumpiness and depression anything to do with your wife's condition? Or is it to do with your daughter? A bit of both, perhaps?'

Why not tell him the truth, Reg thought. Back came the answer; because he'll think I'm off my crust and send me to a psychiatrist.

'Well I do worry about the wife and my girl, of course, but I don't think it's that – or maybe it is, and I just don't realize it.'

Dr Raymond made no move towards his prescription pad. He went on staring at Reg. 'I need to know more, Mr Smith.'

'There's not a lot else I can tell you.'

'You have to realize that unless we tackle the cause of the trouble, we won't be able to do more than treat the symptoms – and only for a short time, at that. The trouble, the root cause, will still be there.'

Reg sighed, and in that instant Dr Raymond narrowed his eyes, like a hunter spotting his prey.

'It's not an easy thing to talk about,' Reg said.

'Try, anyway.'

Reg tried. At first he wanted the doctor to believe he was in control of his affliction, that he could live with it, the same way a man could withstand a nagging toothache. 'But naturally I'd sooner be without it altogether.'

'If you'll forgive me saying so,' Dr Raymond murmured, 'I can't imagine a fear of death being a small matter. And I can't believe, either, that a man in your physical condition is coping with his trouble.'

Reg frowned. 'You haven't examined me . . .'

'I don't need to. The last time I saw you, I saw an entirely different man. Even if I hadn't that memory for comparison, I'd say, looking at you, that your nerves are in shreds. Am I right?'

Reg shrugged. 'More or less.'

'Right, now we're getting somewhere.' The doctor clasped his hands and leaned forward. 'Tell me how the attacks, the panics, take you.'

Reg explained that it was exactly the way his wife was with spiders. She hated even seeing them, but if there was one up in the corner of the room, she couldn't stop herself looking at it, even though the experience distressed her. 'I know now that if I think about dying – the certainty, you know? – I'll go stiff with fright. But I can't help doing it. I don't try to do it, it's a . . . well, it's like I'm being . . .'

'Compelled?'

Reg nodded. 'I don't get used to any part of it, either. I'm frightened rigid at the thought that I can't get away from it happening one day, me dying . . .'

The doctor sat back. 'The fear of death is in most people, even the ones who believe there's something else to come afterwards. I take it you don't believe in an after-life?'

112

'I've tried to. It would be a comfort if I could.'

'Can I also take it that you came here thinking I'd believe you were mentally disturbed if you told me the whole truth?'

'Yes, I did.'

'Well I do think you're disturbed, Mr Smith. But you're not unbalanced. What's happened is that a natural dread, which most people keep well governed, has escaped your control. Have you given any thought to the cause?'

Reg told Dr Raymond that he believed his ruined hopes for Mary had left him with no source of pleasure or diversion in his life. 'I love the family I have, but without Mary they don't . . .' He struggled to find the word. 'They don't sustain me.'

'So, in the words of the song, you're tired of living but scared of dying.'

'That's near enough it, I suppose.'

Dr Raymond sat in silence for a minute, staring at the desk. 'The cause of all this distress, then, is the loss of your daughter. I understand you've tried to find her. Are you still trying?'

'No.'

'Why not?'

'Because I know if I ever found her, she would only come back if she was forced. She doesn't *want* to be with us. I can't make her want to.'

'And that's what hurts most. Not being wanted.'

'It's what's most depressing, I think,' Reg said.

'I think you're looking at it the wrong way, Mr Smith. Have you any reason to believe she doesn't love you?'

Reg shrugged. 'If she'd anything like the love I have for her she'd have stayed, wouldn't she?'

'Not necessarily. I'd say two things to you, Mr Smith. The first is this – it's entirely possible that she didn't love you the less, she simply loved the idea of freedom more, and it may be no fault of yours that she needed to run away. Secondly, bear in mind that if you want to keep something, you have to let a lot of it go.'

Five minutes later Reg left the surgery. He had been given no prescription to help him, other than the doctor's words. By the time he reached the windy corner of the street, he decided he had been helped tremendously. He definitely felt better.

He stopped on the corner, looked at the pub across the road and decided he would have a pint. Without being sure of the why or wherefore, he felt there was something to celebrate.

Before half of the pint was gone Reg had come to a firm decision. He would start looking for Mary again. When he found her he would tell her how much he loved her and that he wanted to help her in any way he could – and he would make it clear he wasn't going to try to make her come home again. That way, he believed, she could still be his beloved daughter, still his friend, and she'd have proof of his feelings, for he would respect her need to be free. There was always the hope, too, that if he didn't fall out with her she might just come home one day, of her own free will.

Reg finished his beer and stood for a minute, gauging how he really felt. It had been no illusion, he decided. He was miles better. He had his confidence back, and his determination was restored, all thanks to a few fog-clearing words from the doctor. As for the fear of dying, he was beginning to wonder how he could have let it get on top of him the way it had. One thing was sure – it would never happen again. How could he be preoccupied with death when he had so much now to occupy him and distract him?

* * *

Two days after Reg's visit to the doctor Mary found herself in a consulting room, too. It was barer than the place Reg had gone to and there was no discernible atmosphere of friendliness or understanding. Mary hadn't wanted to come but one of the other girls with the band, Tina, had talked her into it.

The first thing Mary noticed was how thin the walls were. She could hear people talking in the rooms on either side. As she sat on the trolley-bed, wrapped in a scratchy white gown and nothing else, she wondered what would happen if they found out the name and address she had given were false. Tina said it was all right, girls came here all the time and never gave their real names. But that was easy for Tina to say, Mary thought – she didn't have to do it, and she didn't have to sit here waiting for somebody to start poking about, either.

Mary jumped as the door rattled open and the doctor came in, followed by a glum-faced nurse in a baggy striped dress.

'Hello, hello,' the doctor said absently, not looking at Mary but studying the nurse's writing at the top of the case card he was carrying. 'Miss Young, is it?'

'Yes,' Mary said, feeling a blush.

'Right then. Lie down there, will you, and we'll have a look.'

Mary lay back along the length of the trolley, feeling herself tremble as the nurse arranged her legs and wheeled forward an instrument tray.

'Don't worry about a thing,' the doctor murmured, pulling on rubber gloves and picking up something that looked like a short trumpet with a handle on its side. He shook back his straggly grey hair and moved close, so that Mary could only see his head between her spread knees. 'It won't hurt. Try and relax.'

It did hurt. Mary set her teeth and shut her eyes tightly. The thing probed around inside her and then it widened, hurting her even more. She bit her lip but a little grunt escaped her. Why had she come here? Everything would have cleared up with the salt-water baths, she was sure of that.

'Cervix reddish,' the doctor intoned. The nurse wrote on the card. 'Slight mucopurulent discharge.'

Mary felt a hand pressing down on the bony arch at the front of her pelvis.

'Pus expressible from the urethra on pressure against the symphisis pubis.'

Now the doctor was uncapping a bottle, or that was what it sounded like. A moment later Mary felt something else moving around inside her.

'Just taking a swab,' the doctor grunted. When he had finished he put the swab back in its tube, recapped it, then moved back and removed the painful instrument. 'That's that, Miss Young. You can get up now.'

Hugging herself, Mary sat up and swung her legs over the side of the trolley. She hoped that was it. She wanted out of there before they found some other way to hurt her.

The doctor pulled off his gloves and threw them into a wheeled enamel bucket. 'Well now, young woman.' He turned to Mary. He was frowning, though not severely. 'Do you know what NSU is?'

'I think I've heard of it,' Mary said.

'It's what you've got. It's a venereal infection. Venereal means something passed on by the act of sex. I've no doubt you know what sex is.'

The nurse made a half smile, though her face remained glum.

'The general theory around these parts, Miss Young,

116

and around the rest of the country as far as I can gather, is that you bring your venereal troubles to a clinic like this, you get them identified, and then you get them cured. That's all there is to it.' The doctor cocked his head. 'Is that what you've heard?'

'I – I'm not sure . . .' Mary had been told they would give her some tablets and within a week or two her soreness and the discharge would clear up.

'Well, I'm pretty confident we can cure you,' the doctor said. 'This time. And maybe the next time, if you're foolish enough to let this happen again. But you should know this – some people are disfigured for life by venereal infections. And there's a whole host of other diseases that can spring from this one, and some of them aren't curable at all.'

Mary nodded, using her old school technique of letting the lecture exhaust itself around her ears.

'You must take greater precautions, because you're putting your health at severe risk. Tell me, are you on the pill?'

'No.'

'Well get on it as fast as you can. Do you have a family doctor?'

For a moment Mary wondered what to say, then she nodded.

'Talk to him about it. Don't waste any time. Now, another thing. You'll have to let us know who your partner is.'

Mary frowned. 'Sorry?'

'Your boyfriend. The man you've been sleeping with. He may need treatment, too. Can you give us his name and address? It'll all be in confidence, I promise you.'

Mary swallowed hard. She couldn't tell them it was

Chris. She didn't dare tell them anybody's name or she'd be in trouble with the band. 'I don't know who it was.'

'You didn't *know*?'

'No. It was just . . .' Mary swallowed again. 'Somebody at a party. He came from somewhere else, he was a visitor.'

The doctor drummed flattened fingers on his chest. 'Do you know anybody who might know him, then? I mean there must have been somebody at the party who knew him, invited him.'

'He was a gatecrasher.'

'Look, if you're protecting somebody, don't. You'll do him no favours. The man will need medical treatment, it's very important that he has it.'

'I told you – I don't know who he was.'

The doctor turned away, sighing. 'You can get dressed now,' he said. 'Nurse will give you some tablets. See you take them all, then come back in two weeks and we'll have a look at you.' He left without another word and without looking at Mary again.

Ten minutes later she was out on the street again with a bottle of tetracycline tablets in her pocket and an appointment card bearing a date she couldn't read. Which didn't matter anyway. She wouldn't be going back.

She hurried along to the guest house where the band were staying, relieved that at least she had some medicine and that the infection would soon be gone. All she had to worry about now was Chris finding out. She was pretty sure she had caught the infection from him, since he'd been the only one to touch her for more than a month. If it had been him she didn't care. She loved him. She would do anything for him and she would pay any price for loving him.

'He mustn't get to know,' she muttered through chattering teeth. He might not want to know her any more if he found out she had an infection. Mary groaned. To be rejected by Chris was unthinkable. It had taken every effort and wile she could think of to get him to respond to her. She couldn't, she just *couldn't* let a silly little thing like an infection ruin everything.

11

Towards the end of 1981 the British pop chart-topper was *Every Little Thing She Does is Magic*, by the Police. A year later, a thing called *Save Your Love* was at the top, sung by a 'fifties-type duo called Renée and Renata.

'Music's dying,' Tina said to Zoe and Carla as they sat down in the Leamington Spa Macdonald's to share two Big Macs and two coffees between them.

'Me and music both,' Carla murmured. 'I'm knackered. These all-night thrashes are getting too much for me.'

'But what about it, really?' Tina said.

'What about what?' Zoe asked.

'The bloody music scene. I mean the charts are supposed to be some indication of the way music's going, right? So what's up there at number one? Some fat Italian geezer and a bird in a Come Dancing number, twittering about saving their love. Christ.'

'Yeah,' Zoe sighed, staring at the food. 'Tear us off my share of that burger, will you? Every time I try it I get ketchup halfway up my arms.'

With strong, slender black fingers Tina ripped the bun in two and sat a piece on a napkin in front of Zoe. 'Chris and Mike were saying how the pendulum's swinging again. Going back to the way things were, you know? Mike says people are never going to be revolution minded. They don't want change, they just want the same old rotation.'

Zoe sniffed. 'They weren't talking that way at the end of 1980, were they? It was all the big chat then, about how Giro Ripoff was going to revolutionise the scene and put the backbone into music – and it was going to be music that had the power to change people's thinking and their way of doing things. Shit. When I think of it. The sky was going to be the limit. Look at us now. Doing gigs for buttons and having to live on one meal a day – if you can call this a meal.'

They looked at each other, the one-time envy of thousands of girls, the chicks who went everywhere with the band. Their outlooks had changed as much as their circumstances. Tina, tall, black and lithe, once aspiring to a career as a dancer, had now settled for the slim hope of marriage as soon as she found the right kind of man – steady, hard-working and with a job that wasn't going to be Thatchered out from under him. Zoe, whose dyed and frizzed hair had become her trademark even though she didn't like the colour or style any more, planned to make her peace with the DHSS, soon, and get properly on the dole. After that she hoped to find a job and stick at it until somebody came along who would marry her and look after her. Carla, who had once compared herself to Cher, only younger, wanted to go back to her parents in Ireland, if they would have her.

'We could have done worse,' Tina said through a mouthful of bun. 'I mean the guys have been good to us, when you think about it. There's plenty that would have ditched us long ago.'

'They've got dependent on us,' Zoe said. 'Like wives. We do the lot for them, don't we? For bugger-all wages. Who else would do the things they expect us to do? This week alone I've had to let the guy in the printers touch me up something chronic, just so we could get an extra five hundred handbills for nothing. Then I'd to pinch a bottle of Scotch each for Sam and Dave because the sods are turning into alcoholics, and there was all that washing and ironing I did, too. Piles of it. All for nothing.'

'All for the glory of being family,' Carla drawled. 'It won't last much longer. Best thing to do is put your memories away safely, the good ones, so you can run through them when you're a granny.'

'Do you think the band'll break up?' Zoe asked.

Carla shook her head. 'Not until they're too old to squeeze into their leathers. They still have a following, and it'll stick. They're just not flavour of the month any more, that's all. They'll scrape by. They'll have to, they'd evaporate if they broke up.'

'That's right,' Tina said. 'They're useless without each other. Like bees. Got to work as a team or they can't work at all. They can't even go for a pee on their own, it's got to be a group activity.'

'Bloody hell,' Carla murmured, staring across at the counter. 'Look who's come into money.'

They turned and saw Mary handing over a fiver to pay for two burgers and a coffee the assistant had put in front of her. As she came towards the girls Zoe reached across and slid a chair out from another table and edged it into place beside her.

'Take the weight off, Chuck.'

'Ta, Zoe.' Mary sat down and immediately began tearing the wrapper off one of the buns. 'I'm flaming starving.'

'Where'd you get the cash, then?' Tina asked her. 'You were skint this morning.'

Mary smiled secretively. 'I've got my ways.'

'Well share the secret with us, for God's sake,' Zoe said. 'It's been a long time since any of us had more than a couple of quid to play with at once.'

Mary uncapped her coffee and took a bite from her

burger. She chewed for a minute, swallowed some coffee then jerked her head towards the window. 'Know that big stationers shop down there by the traffic lights? I went in there with a carrier bag stuffed with bits of cardboard, all bent up to make the bag look really full. But there was all this space in it, see?'

'So what did you do?' Zoe demanded. 'Empty a till into it?'

'I nicked a couple of books, really posh ones, with padded leather covers and gold round the edges. It was dead easy. If I'd had a bigger bag I could have got more.'

Carla was frowning. 'What did you nick books for?'

'Because there's a shop round the corner that buys them second hand. The bloke gave me a funny look when I put them on the counter, but I told him they were a present that I didn't want, because I'd got them at home already.'

'He swallowed a story like that from a bird in punk gear?'

Carla shook her head. 'He must be thick as two planks.'

'Nah,' Zoe said. 'Lots of students dress that way now. And there's a lot of students in this town.' She looked at Mary. 'How much did the guy give you?'

'Ten quid.'

'*Ten?*'

'Yeah.'

Zoe rolled her eyes. 'I'm going to get myself a plastic bag in a minute. I could use some Christmas shopping money.'

Mary took out her little plastic purse, removed three pound notes and placed one in front of each of the girls. 'There you are. Happy Christmas.'

The girls snatched up the money, offering profuse thanks.

123

'You're a good scout, Mary,' Zoe said.

'Yeah.' Carla kissed the pound note before she pocketed it. 'You're one of the best, kid.'

Mary was blushing. 'You deserve it,' she said. 'All of you. You've been good to me. Especially this last six months.'

At the beginning of July Mary developed pleurisy. Throughout the time she was in hospital, the girls visited her daily; they also handled her cover story, confirming to the hospital authorities that she was Tracy Young and that she lived rough and had no family.

When she left hospital, weak and still rather ill, Tina, Carla and Zoe nursed her until she was well again. By that time, all four had become as close as any real family, and a good deal closer than many.

'I'm going to spend my quid on ten decent fags and a bar of chocolate,' Carla said. 'The way we've been living lately, I'm due a bit of luxury.'

'I can get some mascara,' Zoe said. 'And if I've any money left over, I'll – ' She stopped, noticing the expression on Tina's face. Her eyes were fixed on the door and she was lowering her head, as if she wanted to hide. 'What's up, Tina?'

'I think it's the filth. Guy in a raincoat over there. He came in a minute ago and he's stood there watching Mary ever since.'

'Oh, God, no . . .' Mary stiffened, not daring to look. 'I was sure nobody saw me.'

'Maybe the guy in the bookshop gave him your description,' Tina murmured.

Zoe had turned her head a fraction, just far enough to see the man without appearing to look at him. 'He's got the look of a cop about him, right enough,' she whispered.

'And he's really staring. Christ, what are we going to do?'

'We can't run for it,' Carla moaned. 'Not unless somebody knows where the back door is.'

Mary put her clenched hands on the table, the knuckles white. 'You three just walk out. It's me he wants.'

'Don't be soft,' Zoe hissed. 'If one of us is in it, we're all in it. And don't argue.'

'Maybe we could rush him,' Tina suggested. 'You know, just go right over there, knock him on his back and beat it fast.'

'Oh shit!' Zoe hissed. 'He's coming over!'

Like statues they sat staring across the table at each other as the man came forward. He stopped beside Mary and bent down.

'All right if I talk to you for a minute or two, love?'

Mary's head jerked round. She stared into his face. 'Dad. What're you doing here?'

Everybody relaxed.

'I'm on a stopover in Coventry,' Reg said. 'I saw an advert for the concerts here tonight and tomorrow, so I popped over on the chance I might see you.' He looked at the other girls and nodded. 'If I'm disturbing anything, maybe I could see you after . . .'

'We're just going,' Tina said quickly.

'Yeah.' Zoe pushed back her chair and stood up. 'We've tons to do.'

Carla and Tina got up, smiling reassuringly at Mary. 'We'll catch up with you later on,' Carla said.

Mary nodded uneasily. 'Right. See you.'

When the girls had gone Reg sat down opposite Mary, smiling at her steadily. 'It's been over a year,' he said. 'How have you been, love?'

'I've been fine.'

'You look a bit peaky. Been eating properly, have you?'

'How did you find me?'

Reg reached across the table and patted Mary's hand. 'Any time I've tried to get in touch with you, I've either gone to the theatre if there was a concert on, or I've made a tour of the hamburger places. Today I got lucky. I've turned up at quite a few places the band's been over the last year or so. But I never even saw you. I was beginning to think you'd given them up.'

'I don't always go to the concerts,' Mary said.

'But you go round with the band, do you?'

Mary nodded.

'It's not the life I'd have picked for you. I'd all those plans to get you a job, see you fixed up . . .'

'I'm not coming home, Dad.'

'I know that. And I'm not going to try and make you.' Reg's fingers tightened on Mary's for an instant, then he drew back. 'I came because I wanted to see you and know you're all right. And I wanted to tell you I always think of you, and I'll always be there if you need me.' He pointed at the cup in front of Mary. 'Do you want another coffee?'

'No, this'll do me.' Mary's face had softened and lost its defensive look. She cleared her throat softly. 'It's nice to see you, Dad. I think about you a lot.'

'Good. I'm glad.'

'How's Mum and the boys?'

'They're all right. They miss you in their different ways, of course. But they're fine.' Reg picked up the tinfoil ashtray, turned it between his fingers for a minute and laid it down again. He sighed. 'How do things look for the future, Mary?'

126

'Things look OK. I don't like to think too far ahead, though. There's no point, is there?'

'Maybe not.' Reg gazed across at the window. Slanting pale sunlight dappled the pane and put bright spots on the floor tiles. 'It's a lovely day,' he said. 'Do you fancy going for a walk?'

'Like we used to when I was little?'

'That's right, love. But this time I promise I won't hold your hand and embarrass you, or carry you when you get tired.'

They walked slowly down the long Parade, stopping every few minutes outside brightly decorated shop windows, chatting easily as they crossed the Victoria Gardens and stopped on the river bridge leading to the public library.

'I've got to be back in Coventry by three,' Reg said finally. 'And I'm sure there's things you've got to be doing.' He turned to Mary and cupped the side of her face gently with his hand. 'I'm sorry it's been such a short visit, love. But at least I've seen you, and I know you're all right.' He reached into his inside jacket pocket and brought out an envelope. 'Here. It's been getting fatter the longer I've carried it around with me.'

Mary took the envelope and looked inside. There was a thick wad of five pound notes. 'Oh, Dad, I – '

'Now don't tell me you can't take it, because it's *for* you and nobody else. And don't tell me you can't use it, either.'

'But this is such a lot . . .'

'There's never enough, Mary. We could always do with a bit more. Spend that on yourself. It'll please me to know you're doing that.' He touched the shoulder of her thin jacket. 'Maybe get yourself something warm to wear while you're at it.'

Mary put the envelope in her pocket, then she leaned close and kissed Reg on the cheek. 'I love you, Dad.'

'And I adore you, my pet.' Reg blinked three times, rapidly. 'I'd better be on my way before I start bubbling. Are you going to walk with me to the bus stop?'

'Of course I am.'

The last thing Reg asked Mary before he stepped on to the Coventry bus was that she should get in touch with him, at any time at all, if ever she was in trouble. Mary promised she would, and as she walked away from the bus stop she realized she had meant it.

Halfway along the Parade she realized that although it was cold, she didn't want to go back to the digs straight away. Her father's visit, and the pleasantness he'd brought with him, had begun to produce a solitary mood in Mary. For the first time in over a year, she truly felt like being on her own. She turned and walked back down the Parade to the Jephson Memorial Gardens. Taking the path that led down to the cafeteria by the River Leam, she found a bench in a spot which caught the sun and shielded her from the wind. There she sat down and watched the swans begging bread from two old people by the water's edge. As she sat she dreamed and wondered.

When they'd been walking in the town her father had mentioned that Mary didn't seem to have changed much. He would perhaps have thought differently if he had spent more time with her. She was sure she had changed a lot. The girl who had run away from home had been the fiercest kind of enthusiast, an addict of the band, someone who would pursue her dreams over hot coals if necessary. Now she was different. The fire had gone out of her enthusiasm for the band and its music. The love she'd had for Chris had turned out to be misplaced. He wasn't what he had seemed. He was *nothing* like the man

128

she had adored, dreamed about and craved for. In place of that adoration she had nothing but a gap. Her life now was full of gaps, the open sockets left by uprooted dreams.

But Mary was also in a rut. A rut had its comforts, it dictated her direction, even if that meant doing no more than going round in circles. The rut held her, and although there was a spark in her that yearned for change, she hadn't the drive or the will to make change happen.

After a few minutes a dark cloud crept across the sun and the air around her began to chill uncomfortably. She stood and made her way back up along the path, wondering how long it would be until things did change. The band wasn't doing all that well nowadays. There was only one roadie left and they were back to travelling in an old van. Soon, Mary knew, the girls would begin to leave. When would she leave, and how?

And after this stale and crumbled dream, what?

12

In the late spring of 1984 Giro Ripoff were booked to play at a rock festival in Sussex. Their performance was enthusiastically received by the fans, so even though there was very little money from the gig after travel and other costs had been dealt with, the band left the venue that night in a buoyant, boisterous mood.

They had planned to drive overnight to Eastbourne for another open-air event the following day, but when Sam, their gaunt leader, noticed a welcoming-looking inn half an hour into their journey, they turned off the road and parked in the broad forecourt.

'Just a couple of drinks,' Sam promised worried little Mike who, in the absence of road crew, had to shoulder most of the band's travelling and setting-up arrangements.

'Just as long as it's only two, then,' Mike grunted, getting out of the van. 'We can't afford the time or the cash for any more than that.'

Mary and Zoe, the only two girls remaining with the band, had been asleep in the back of the van, exhausted from the work of carrying instruments, cooking, cheerleading, general hustling and reloading the van. Zoe woke up as the others piled out. She nudged Mary.

'They're going for a drink. Coming?'

Mary said she wanted to sleep.

'Aw, come on. It'll be a kind of celebration. We haven't had one of them for a while.'

Wearily Mary followed Zoe across the forecourt, tucking in her shirt and ruffling her hair back into its spiked symmetry. As they went through the door of the bar the sounds from the customers hushed rapidly and died away. They watched as the four leathered, booted and wild-haired young men tramped up to the bar, followed by their two short-skirted girlfriends. By now the band and the girls were well used to this kind of reception. Sam smiled at the scowling barman and ordered the drinks.

'Not the best place for a celebration,' Mary murmured to Zoe.

'No, I suppose not. Too many cravats, cavalry twills and suede shoes.' A man at a nearby table was nudging his friend and smothering a snigger as he stared at Mary's backside in the tight black PVC. Zoe groaned. 'You've made a fan already.'

Mary didn't hear. She was watching Chris. He had been high all day. Now he looked as if he was entering his active phase, the time when his eyes unhooded and he became animated. He was tapping the bar rhythmically with the silver ring on the little finger of his right hand, while the fingers of his other hand twitched to the same tune, one that only he could hear. Perhaps now, Mary thought, she would be able to talk to him. Earlier he had been too high to respond to anything anybody said to him. Mary had wanted to talk to him for two days now, but one thing and another had kept getting in the way.

She sidled closer.

'Is everything cool?' Chris asked, barely glancing at her.

'It could be cooler,' Mary said.

'Have a drink, drown the sorrows, bury the woes.' Chris put on his one-sided smile. 'You can't get out of life alive, so you might as well make the most of it.'

Mary didn't know how many times she had heard that. Chris carted around maybe twenty phrases and they

131

constituted most of what he ever said – when he was in a reasonable mood. At other times he resorted to slanging and threats. Boiled down, he was a very uncomplicated person, though he tried hard to give the opposite impression.

'Can we sit down somewhere and have a talk?' Mary said.

'I don't want to talk.'

Chris had spotted a girl in the corner, sitting with a young man who wore a blazer and flannels. Chris was smiling at the girl now, tilting his head in an enigmatic, questioning way. The young man was trying to ignore Chris. He was also trying to ignore the fact that his girlfriend was responding with a smile of her own.

'Chris, we've got to talk. It's important.'

'Now don't go putting me in a bad mood, Mary. I haven't *got* to do anything. Just pick up your drink, get it inside you and cool things. All right?'

Mary moved away from him and stood beside Zoe again.

'Here.' Zoe handed Mary her glass. 'Cheer up.'

'That's easier said than done.'

'What's the matter?'

Mary hesitated. 'Oh, I've got a problem. I wanted to talk to Chris about it, but he's too busy giving that girl over there the eye.'

'Can you talk to me about it?'

Mary shrugged. 'I suppose I can. But he's the one I should talk to first, really.'

'Uh-oh.' Zoe stared at Mary. 'Not you-know-what, is it?'

'Yeah.'

'Are you sure?'

Mary nodded. 'I am now.'

132

Zoe was about to say something else when the young man in the blazer shot up from his chair and glared at Chris. 'Do you mind?' he demanded. 'This young lady happens to be with me and I take exception to the way you're behaving towards her.'

'Oh bloody hell, swite me,' Sam said as Chris and the otheres began laughing. 'He takes exception, Chris. I should watch my step if I were you.'

'Yeah,' Mike said, 'he'll most likely give you the Chinese burn.'

'I'm warning you,' the young man said, taking a step away from the table.

'Please,' his girlfriend hissed, pink with embarrassment. 'Sit down, Rupert.'

Sam came forward, stark disbelief on his face. 'Rupert? *Rupert?*'

'Looks more like an Algie to me,' Chris said.

'Just watch it!' Rupert spluttered. Everyone in the place was watching him. Conscious of the fact, he found himself with no way to go but forward. 'I want an apology out of you!'

'Don't be silly,' Chris drawled, then winked at the girl.

'Apologize, you hairy swine!' Rupert glanced from side to side, looking for allies. If he had any, they were keeping it a secret. 'Right this instant!'

'Rupert,' Chris said calmly, 'why don't you sit down? You're making an arse of yourself.'

There was a loud crack from the bar. Everyone turned and looked. The barman had brought a truncheon down smartly on the oak top. 'I think you should drink up and go,' he said.

'Christ,' Sam groaned, 'we've only just got here.'

'And you've started making trouble already. So I want you to go.' The barman gestured with the truncheon. 'I

133

know you're mob-handed, but I reckon I can make a few dents with this before you claim any victory.'

Mike was staring at the truncheon. 'That bloody thing's illegal.'

The barman shrugged. 'We can sort out the legal side once I've flattened you with it.' He looked round the room. 'I don't think you'd find many in here that'd testify I ever used it, anyway.'

'Aw, shit,' Sam turned to the others. 'Sup up.'

As they left Chris was noticably agitated. 'I should have popped that little bastard,' he said, pulling open the back door of the van. 'I should have made him eat his brass buttons.'

'No, no,' Sam said placatingly, 'that wouldn't have been fair. I mean, you can see he's due back in Burton's window at midnight.'

The others laughed but Chris didn't. He jumped into the van and threw himself on to a pile of blankets in the corner. 'Pissy little puffed-up arsehole,' he muttered.

Beside the van Zoe tapped Mary on the shoulder. 'Don't talk to him tonight, will you? Not while he's in that mood.'

'I'll have to say something to him some time. I've been trying for two days as it is.'

'Wait till tomorrow. You know what Chris is like if you catch him raw. He goes right over the top.'

'I think I can keep him from doing that,' Mary said. 'He's a lot softer than he makes out.'

'Well, it's your funeral. Don't say I didn't warn you.'

'I won't.'

After an hour of driving, Zoe, Sam and Dave were asleep. Mike and the roadie were in the seats at the front, Mike half-dozing while the roadie took his turn at the wheel. In his corner Chris was still wide awake, muttering to himself at odd moments, glaring at the floor of the van as wedges of street light flickered over the huddled, sleeping, blanket-covered bodies. Mary, who had been curled in the opposite corner to Chris, finally got on all fours and crawled over to him.

'What do you want?' Chris asked her coldly.

'I want to talk.'

'Well I don't.'

'Please, Chris. It's important.'

He drew a breath and let it out very slowly. 'What does it take to make you bugger off?'

That was what he had said just before the last shred of Mary's dream had blown away on a final gust of disappointment. For the best part of two years now, the only attention he'd paid her was when he needed a woman to sleep with and she was the only one available. If only he had ignored her completely during that time, Mary thought, she wouldn't be in this predicament.

'Will you just listen to me for two minutes? *Please.*'

In the half-dark Chris's eyes widened, catching the flashing light. 'When I say bugger off, I mean bugger off!'

'I'm pregnant.'

Chris's voice caught on the edge of a shout. 'What?' he croaked.

'I'm pregnant. I'm going to have a baby.'

'I know what frigging pregnant means!' He pushed himself up on his knees, towering over Mary where she sat. 'What are you telling *me* for?'

'Because it's yours, Chris. Ours.'

'Sod off! Don't think I'm falling for that one! You've had more goes with this entire bloody outfit than any other bird I've met!'

'Not since you,' Mary said, her voice trembling. 'I swear it, Chris – nobody else since you.'

'I'm not buying it!' Chris thrust himself to his feet, bracing his hands on the panels. 'Stop the van!' he yelled. 'Do you hear me? Stop the bloody van!'

Everybody was awake before the driver had pulled in to the side of the road.

'What's all the racket?' Sam demanded, struggling out of his blanket.

'It's this cow! She's trying out the old paternity lark on me! Her, of all people – Mary, Mary, not-so-bloody contrary!' Chris jerked up the handle of the door and swung it open. 'Right! Out you get!' He pushed Mary so violently she stumbled as she landed on the grass verge and fell.

'Take it easy,' Sam shouted. 'There's no need for that.'

'Just leave this to me,' Chris snarled back. He jumped out of the van, grabbed Mary by the elbow and dragged her to her feet. 'Over there, bitch. Move!' He shoved her towards a tree and slammed her back against it. He clamped a hand round her neck and put his face close to hers. 'So just tell me what you thought I'd do about you being in the club.'

'I didn't want you to do anything,' Mary whimpered.

'Then why did you tell me?'

She swallowed against his restraining hand. 'I thought you'd want to know.'

'Like hell I would.' Chris spat on the grass. 'Listen. You knew the deal when you took up with us. No trouble. No waves. The first sign of trouble or hassle and you're out. The rules haven't changed.'

'I'm not giving anybody hassle, Chris . . .'

'What – you're up the spout and you're telling me that? Do me a bloody favour.'

'If I wanted anything, it was just for you to maybe tell me what to do. I'm a bit frightened about it.'

'It's none of my business. I don't want to know. Now have you got that, or do I have to punch it into you?'

'I've got it,' Mary said, feeling her tears break and thinking, in the same instant, *this is it, this is the end*.

'Right,' Chris breathed, releasing her. 'Get yourself back in that van. We'll take you as far as Eastbourne. When we get there you're on your own. You don't follow after us, you don't finger us for anything, you don't come within miles of us ever again. Take me very seriously, Mary. If you don't disappear the minute you get out of the van then you'll be one sad, bruised little chick. Do you understand what I've said?'

Mary nodded, her shoulders quaking. She climbed into the van ahead of Chris, seeing the faces of the others pale in the roadside light, already as distant as strangers.

'Time heals nothing, my friend,' the old man said, breathing fishily in the face of a young policeman. 'Time erodes. That's its function. Time *rots* everything. Your memories, your spirit, your very body. Time is the ultimate enemy.'

'And it's time you were in bed, if you've got one,' the policeman said. He placed a cautious hand on the old man's ragged collar and peered into his eyes. They were dull and pink-rimmed, weary brown discs that didn't appear to focus. 'Do you live near here?'

'I live wherever I happen to be.'

'In that case you're lucky it's a warm night.'

'I never feel the cold, officer. I'm a philosopher, you see. I've rationalized the cold. It's nothing but an absence of heat. What I've rationalized cannot hurt me.'

The policeman nodded and moved away, leaving the old man standing on the corner staring distractedly at the traffic. When he had walked ten yards the constable stopped and turned, making sure the old fellow hadn't fallen on to the road. Strictly speaking he should have been taken in, because he was arguably drunk and incapable; but if the policeman did that the night sergeant – a man who didn't like to be disturbed – would develop a grudge, and a vindictive superior officer was the last thing a young constable needed.

At a boarded-up shop he stopped again and shone his torch between the planks across the broken window. He saw a rat scamper through the beam and he switched off the torch abruptly. He hated rats.

'Excuse me . . .'

Still unnerved by the sight of the rat the policeman turned abruptly, frowning. A girl was standing beside him. She was thin and untidy-looking, like a dozen or so he saw every night, roaming the streets alone or in drab little groups.

'What can I do for you?'

'I'm looking for the hostel.'

'What hostel? There's a lot of hostels in Camberwell.'

'The girls' hostel. A man outside the tube told me it was down here somewhere.'

The policeman nodded. 'Just over there,' he said, pointing to a building on the opposite corner. 'The door with the light above it.'

'Thanks.'

'Just arrived in London, have you?'

'Yeah. Well, yesterday I got here.'

'From the North, by the sound of you.'

'That's right.' The girl glanced across the road as she switched her holdall from one hand to the other. 'Can you tell me what I do when I go over there? I've not been to a hostel before.'

'The woman at the desk'll explain everything to you.'

'Right. Thanks very much.'

The policeman watched her cross the road. He wondered about his own daughter, still only three. Could that happen to her? Could his beloved child become so alienated from her family that she'd wind up in London's army of teenage down-and-outs? He began walking again, driving the notion from his head.

At the foot of the hostel steps Mary put down her bag and drew her fingers through her hair, wishing she had a mirror. As she stood there two girls came along the pavement and went up the steps. Mary grabbed her holdall and followed them.

The reception desk was narrow and poorly lit. Behind it a woman in a dark blue overall was leaning on the wall, reading a newspaper. She glanced up as the two girls walked past. She nodded to them, then switched her dull gaze on Mary.

'Yes?'

Mary wet her lips. 'I'm wondering if I could book in for the night, please.'

'No, you can't. We're full.'

'Oh. I see.' Thoughts of the previous night flooded forward. The cold, the discomfort of the railway station bench she slept on, the man who'd tried to interfere with her. 'Could you tell me the address of another place?'

The woman snatched up a leaflet and handed it over. 'All the places are on there.'

Mary stared at it. 'Is there one near here?'

'The addresses are all printed down there,' the woman snapped. She picked up her newspaper and leaned back on the wall again.

'Thanks a lot.'

Out on the street Mary spent five frantic minutes under a lamp post, struggling to decipher the printing on the leaflet. Nothing would come to her. All she saw were strings of letters. An occasional word looked familiar, and there was one she was sure of – 'Catholic'. But in all the leaflet made no sense. It was like being a foreigner, lost and not able to speak the language. Mary began to panic. She didn't want to spend another night in the open.

'What's the trouble?'

She looked up and saw a young man. 'Pardon?'

'You look kind of distressed,' he said. He was pleasant-faced, well-dressed and didn't seem to pose any threat. Something in his eyes reminded Mary of her father.

'I'm trying to find a hostel. That one over there's full.'

'Oh.' The young man shook his head. 'I don't know much about hostels, I'm afraid.' He pointed to the leaflet. 'Have you got some addresses there?'

'Uhuh.'

'Is it directions you need, or what?'

'Not exactly.' Mary looked at the leaflet again, then sighed. 'What it is – well, I can't read this.'

The young man wrinkled his forehead. 'How do you mean?'

'I can't read it. I can't read anything.' She had never admitted it to anyone before. She'd never had to.

The young man took the leaflet from her and looked at it for a minute. 'Well,' he said finally, 'there are two kinds of hostel listed here – the ones where you pay, and the ones that are free.'

'I didn't know you had to pay in any of them.'

'I don't think they charge very much.'

'I don't have very much,' Mary said. 'Is there a free one near here?'

He looked at the leaflet again and nodded. 'Two. One's for men only, the other one's a Catholic Help Centre.'

140

'I'd better try that one, then. Could you show me where it is?'

'Sure. It's only three or four minutes' walk.'

When they got there Mary stood and gazed up at the stark frontage with its blackened brick and dark-curtained windows. 'Doesn't look very inviting,' she murmured.

'I'm sure it'll be all right inside.'

'Yeah, well I hope so.' Mary turned to the young man. 'Thanks for your help, anyway.'

'That's all right. It's my job, helping people. Well, my part-time job, anyway. Here . . .' He took a card from his pocket and handed it to Mary. 'If I can ever help – oh, I'm sorry.'

'It's all right, I can get somebody to read it to me, if I need to.' Mary looked at the card. 'Is that a phone number at the bottom?'

'Yes, it is.'

'I'm all right with numbers. What is it you do, anyway?'

'I'm with the Samaritans. We're people you ring if you're in trouble, or feeling desperate, or just a bit lost.'

'I'll hang on to the card, then,' Mary said, trying to make it sound jokey.

'Yes, do that. Best of luck at the hostel. I hope things work out for you.'

Mary returned his little wave and turned to face the hostel door. It was halfway open. She stepped forward and pushed. The door creaked open a little wider. She put her head round the side. There was a green-and-yellow painted corridor with notice boards screwed to it at intervals. No one was in sight. Mary stepped inside and cleared her throat loudly, hoping to attract some attention. Somewhere far off she could hear voices. After a minute she began walking towards the sound.

She jumped as a door halfway along the corridor

opened and a nun came out. The two stood looking at one another. The nun had a face like a pink, wizened apple.

'Can I help you?' she asked Mary.

'I was wondering if I could book in – if you're not full, that is.'

'You'll have to go to Reception.' The nun pointed to a sign at the end of the corridor. 'Follow the arrow.'

Mary thanked her and moved on, feeling the little eyes on her back. She found the reception desk and tapped the brass bell. Another nun appeared, much younger than the other one. She asked if she could help and Mary explained that she was looking for accommodation.

'We're not a hotel,' the nun said. 'Our job is to provide help for young women who are in trouble. *Are* you in trouble?'

Again Mary experienced a flooding scenario of a night living rough in London. 'Yes,' she said, suddenly determined to convince this hooded woman that there was no one in more trouble than Mary Smith.

'Would you care to tell me about it?'

'I've got nowhere to live,' Mary said, 'I've no money and no family to go to. I haven't eaten for days and I keep getting these fainting turns.'

The nun appeared to be unmoved. 'It's easy enough to tell me all that. I don't actually know it's true, do I?'

'It's true, all right. And that's not all – I'm pregnant, too.'

Now the nun's expression changed. 'How long have you been pregnant?'

'I'm not sure. About two months, I suppose.'

'I see. Tell me, are you a Catholic?'

'Yes, Sister.'

The nun drummed her fingers on the desk for a few

seconds, then she pointed to the door behind her. 'Go through there and sit down. Someone will come in to see you in a few minutes.'

The few minutes turned out to be nearly half an hour. In that time Mary ran over the events of the past thirty-six hours again and again, wondering if there was anything better she could have done, any alternative path that might have held more promise.

She doubted it. After being abandoned on the front at Eastbourne she had wandered aimlessly for an hour, stunned, unable to believe what had happened to her. Then at mid-morning she began to feel hungry, and with hunger came a starker awareness of her position. All she possessed in the world was right there with her – the holdall jammed with her clothes, and in her purse fifteen pounds Sam had slipped her, plus the fiver Zoe had tearfully begged her to take. In short she had practically nothing, and she had no place to go. She was grounded.

She thought about going home, but rejected the idea. It would be worse there than it had ever been, now that she was pregnant. Her mother would tell her how she had shamed the family and she would never let up about it. Mary didn't want her child being born into that kind of place, anyway.

So where would she go?

She thought about London and the more she thought of it the more the idea appealed to her. Other girls had talked to her about how easy it was to make it in the Smoke; there were more opportunities there, and a girl could be properly anonymous. There was even some glamour in the notion.

The tinge of glamour disappeared during her first three hours in London. For a start she was lost. Vague, long-ago tales of walking up to a crowd of kids somewhere and being welcomed into the family seemed unlikely now. The city felt hostile. The only young bunch she saw all afternoon was a quartet of degenerates slouching around Waterloo Station. Mary imagined that the first thing they'd do, after inviting her to join up with them, would be to gang-bang her and steal her money.

By evening most of her money was gone. London cost a fortune. After wandering the streets until it was dark, making herself available to opportunity, she trudged wearily back to Waterloo Station, found an out-of-the-way bench and decided to stay on it until morning. It was the most uncomfortable night of her life; she even woke at one point to find an old man in a smelly overcoat fumbling with her clothes. She had to scream and swear at him before he would stop.

In the morning she decided to try somewhere further out from the centre, some area where friendly working people lived, a place where she could find the right slot. *Somebody* was bound to help. Zoe had said it time and again – if you just went somewhere, something would turn up. After a coffee and a quick wash in the station Ladies, Mary bought an Underground ticket for Camberwell, because at a gig once she'd met a very friendly girl who came from there. But after another day's wandering she had fared no better in Camberwell than she had around Waterloo. The East End seemed to have its back to her.

So here she was, waiting to be admitted to a Catholic Help Centre. She couldn't imagine there was anything she might have done to make things turn out any better. Grateful at least to be indoors for a spell, she sat breathing the musty air of the bare little room, waiting for fate to make its next move.

When Father Richmond walked into the room he

144

weighed up the girl with one long, hard look. None of the young women who came here ever fooled Father Richmond. What he saw straight away were a girl's weaknesses, like limpets on whatever strengths she possessed, depleting them. Twenty years of assessing the little witches had given the priest an eye as sharp as an angel's own, he often thought,

'Well now,' he said, showing her his impressively firm face, his strong mouth neither smiling nor scowling above his sparkling white dog collar. 'Were you never taught to stand up for a priest?'

Mary stood so abruptly she forgot to take the holdall off her knees and it landed at the priest's feet with a thump. Blushing, she picked it up and put it behind her.

'What is your name, girl?'

'Mary Smith.'

He didn't believe that for a start. Smith, indeed. She could have done better if she was a better liar, but she was the sloppy kind. Even her falsehoods were sloppy.

'I am Father Richmond. It's my job to ascertain if you qualify to be admitted to this centre.'

He crossed to the little writing table by the wall and sat down. The nun from reception came in and closed the door. She made no move to sit, even though there were four chairs in the room. She remained by the door, her hands folded, gazing at the linoleum with distant eyes.

'You can sit down again,' Father Richmond told Mary. He watched her face as she lowered herself to the chair. Shifty eyes, he thought, and a weak mouth. Everything about the girl betokened laxity and weakness of will. 'You say you have no parents?'

'No, Father. They're both dead.'

'Have you any relatives at all?'

'No, I've none. No friends either.'

145

Father Richmond believed that might be true. She had the vapid look of the orphan. But being an orphan excused no one the duty of living a morally spotless life. A person could be penniless, exiled and without family, but that person was still capable of being a decent human being. God gave every man and woman the choice.

'How have you been supporting yourself?'

Mary hesitated. 'I've done odd jobs, just going from place to place, picking up what I could – to live on, like.'

'And why have you stopped doing that?'

'Well, since I got pregnant it's been harder. I feel so ill all the time, and I get these fainting turns – '

'What about your unborn child's father? Has he not offered to help you?'

'No.'

'Does he know you're pregnant?'

'No,' Mary said. 'I shouldn't think so. I don't know who he is, you see.'

Beastly lustings, turpitude, immoral foulness – the priest could detect them all, festering away in that weak skull and whorish body. He could even picture the little strumpet at her work of lewd seduction, preying on some moral midget, sweating and grunting, straddling . . .

'Are you aware that it is a sin to have sexual intercourse before marriage?'

'Yes, Father.'

'Yet you ignored your Church's teaching. You flouted God's law.'

'Yes, Father.'

There were so many of them, Father Richmond thought, girls like this one, so obsessed with corruption that even the fear of damnation wouldn't deter them. He wondered how many men she had lain with. It was a

146

question he might well ask her in the confessional – and find himself shocked by the reply, as he so often was.

'Mary Smith, if you are admitted to this centre you will be required to live by the rules. They are severe rules, aimed at correcting your waywardness. If those rules are in any way breached you will do penance. You will be given work to do, and in all matters you will obey the instructions of the sisters. Do you understand all that?'

'Yes, Father.'

'In return for your work and your obedience you will be fed, sheltered, clothed and provided with medical attention.' Father Richmond stood up. 'Sister Adele will ask you some further questions, for our records, then you'll be shown to the dormitory.'

He gave Mary one more hard look, again impressing his strength on her, then left the room. At a measured pace he walked along the corridor to his office, let himself in and sat down behind the lamplit desk. With hands folded on the blotter he looked at the picture of the martyred St Anthony above the door, and sighed. There were times when he felt like that himself; tortured – mercilessly tormented by the terrible knowledge of sin he bore, the hideous encounters with morally weak young women, day in, day out.

But it was his duty, he reminded himself. It was a feature of his calling and he had no choice but to obey God's will. Liberal priests, young men most of them, insisted that true evil, *foul* evil, did not really exist. But Father Richmond knew better than that. Foul, putrescent evil did exist, and it found its perfect host in young women. His experience was his proof, and so were the scars on his immortal soul.

* * *

'That Father Richmond's bleedin' cracked,' the girl in the next bed told Mary. She was called Agnes and in a lot of ways she reminded Mary of Zoe. 'In fact he's worse than just cracked. If he didn't have us to get his jollies with – you know, asking mucky questions an' such – I reckon he'd be a monster or a rapist or somethin' bent like that.'

At first the dormitory had intimidated Mary. There were so many beds it looked like a hospital ward, but without the screens. There was no privacy. However, after a few minutes, when she realized she wasn't going to be treated like some outsider or newcomer and that no one was paying much attention to her, she began to relax. The bed was comfortable, miles better than a bench, and she had the prospect of breakfast when she woke up. She wasn't sure if she had landed on her feet or not, but she was sure she could have done a lot worse.

'Is the work here hard?' she asked Agnes.

'More borin' than hard, actually. But you get used to it. Well, some girls do. Others crack up, for some reason. It's the screws, I suppose. A lot of kids can't take the pressure.'

'Screws?'

'The nuns. They lean on some girls more than others. When they feel like it they can be right bastards, pardon my French.'

'Do you think I'm the kind they'd lean on?' Mary asked.

'Dunno. Have you been on the game?'

'No.'

'Are you pregnant?'

'Yes, I am.'

'Depend on it, then,' Agnes said. 'They'll lean on you.'

13

Christmas was past, Clara knew, because she had seen them taking down the coloured lights from the lamp posts and changing the window displays in the shops, and for a while the rubbish bins had been filled with crushed tinsel, multi-coloured crêpe paper, broken glass balls and all the other paraphernalia of a dead and gone festive season. Clara didn't remember Christmas itself, she never remembered much for any length of time, but she could be sure it was over. And she was glad it was over. Life was hard enough, but at Christmas it was always that bit harder. Clara believed that when she died, it would be at Christmas.

The weather was cold, bone-chilling cold, and the chilblains on Clara's knuckles and feet throbbed worse than her sciatica; nevertheless it had been a good morning for her. She had scavenged for three hours with her two oilskin shopping bags and by noon they were crammed. At the back of a hotel she had found half a loaf – not even stale – and some broken cakes wrapped in a length of paper towel. Three pints of milk had been sitting on a shop doorstep just waiting to be lifted, and in a dustbin jammed with empty bottles she had found one half-full of wine. Other trash cans had yielded non-edibles such as a woolly hat, one mitten, a transistor radio that actually worked, a penknife and two tea plates that were hardly chipped at all. Among the ashtray debris in a restaurant bin she had unearthed enough half-smoked cigarettes to make a dozen or more roll-ups.

'We'll have us a dinner and a half,' Clara told Mary when she got back to the house. Technically it *was* a house, with a roof, walls, windows and doorways. There was no glass left in the windows and all but two of the doors were gone. Most of the floorboards had been torn up to make fires and the inner walls had great gaps in them, but it was shelter and nobody gave them any trouble there, so in Clara's view they were doing very nicely. It was certainly better than having to wander around all day in the freezing weather, and having to find a warm grating at night, or a cardboard box to sleep in. 'You'll soon warm up when I do you some boiled milk with chunks of bread in it, lovey. My Mum used to give me that when I was a girl. Good for the bones it is. Just you wait till you've got some inside you.'

Mary was sitting on an upended plastic milk crate, hunched forward over a makeshift brazier that produced more smoke than heat. She was wrapped in an old brown overcoat tied at the waist with string. Her hair was matted and her face was smoke-smudged. She squinted through the screen of smoke as the old woman hobbled across with her shopping bags and dumped them on the floor.

'What is it today, Clara?'

'Tuesday, I think. No, Wednesday. It has to be Wednesday. They do the bins up at Schofield's on a Wednesday. They was full yesterday and today they're empty.' Clara sat down on her own milk crate and put one of the shopping bags on her knees. 'Yes, it's Wednesday.'

'Is it a week I've been here, then?'

'Two weeks, nearer.' Clara pulled out the half loaf and held it up like a trophy. 'Look at this! Fresh as anything, too. We'll soon get some of this inside you, with some nice hot milk.'

Mary stared at the dull-glowing fire again. There was

150

Clara and an old man called Percy. They were the ones who lived here, as she remembered. The others she saw were just people who came and went, bringing things, taking things. So it was just her, Clara and Percy; they were the only ones living here. For a while Mary hadn't been sure.

She knew there was something wrong with her. Whole days passed without her doing anything. Sometimes her head throbbed and her skin felt like hot paper and all she could do was lie down. She had been sick a few times, she could remember Clara cleaning her up. And she was never hungry. She ate food when it was there but didn't mind if there was none. Each time she had been sick, it was eating that had done it.

'Where's Percy?'

Clara made a face, deepening the criss-crossing wrinkles on her cheeks and chin. 'He's been bad again,' she said. 'With his chest. Said he was goin' to sit up near the bridge for a while an' get some clean air into his lungs. If you ask me, it's more than his chest that's the trouble. It's his stomach as well.'

Mary felt the mound of her stomach shifting under the coat. The baby was still there, then. It must be getting quite big. She wondered vaguely when it would be born. And where.

'Anybody knows you can't drink meths for long an' get off with it,' Clara said. 'An' there was the time he had half a tin of Brasso. Drank it right off, in one go. Christ, what a do that was. It stands to reason, his stomach's bound to be full of holes.'

Mary remembered stumbling into this house out of the driving sleet. It seemed a very long time ago. She had decided to take off that day, just to get on a train for somewhere. They would have thrown her off when they

151

discovered she'd no ticket, but that wouldn't have mattered. By that time she'd have been somewhere else. But the sleet had started, and she had been very tired anyway. She ran across the waste ground outside looking for a place to shelter, and that was how she had found Clara and Percy.

'I went out for a little walk while you were away, Clara. Didn't get far, though. Only to the corner. I came over all dizzy. Had to get back.'

'You'll feel better with the bread an' milk inside you. Don't fret, lovey.'

Mary had come back not only because walking had made her feel dizzy, but also because she had seen a nun, her habit flapping like the wings of a big bat as she crossed the road. The very sight of nuns scared Mary now. They had been terrible to her in that place. She still had dreams about it, even though it was so long ago. One or two of them had been all right, but there were three in particular who had never let up. They told Mary what a sinner she was, what a loose young woman she had become and probably always would be. They had kept finding extra work for her, and they made her do penances, kneeling on the bare floor for half-an-hour at a time. The priest too, Father Richmond – he had made her confess practically her whole life to him. She had come to dread going into the chapel and shutting herself in that cubicle.

'I was noticin' while I was out,' Clara murmured, 'Christmas must be past. All the decorations is down. I remember seein' them takin' down the lights.'

'Christmas was a while ago.'

'Just as well. I hate Christmas.' Clara got up and fetched a battered aluminium pan from a tea chest in the corner. She put it down by the brazier and fished out a bottle of milk from one of her bags. 'Oh, you're going to love this, Mary. Just you wait.'

She had hit one of the nuns, Mary remembered. It was only a slap, flat on the cheek, but it had made a sudden, sharp sound like a twig being snapped. Something like that was bound to have happened, there had been no way of avoiding it. They drove her too hard, they gave her no peace. They even moved her to the other end of the dormitory when they realized she got on well with Agnes. There were a lot of girls in the place, but the sisters managed to make Mary feel isolated, totally alone at the mercy of their malice. The slap ended everything. Smouldering dislike turned to hysteria; the nun screamed and Mary panicked. She ran straight out of the place, leaving everything behind. She hadn't even taken a coat. She ran and she ran, until she was as far away from the nuns as her feet could carry her.

'Here he comes,' Clara said as a rumbling cough at the doorway fanfared the entry of Percy. 'I better put a bit more milk in the pan.'

'Cold as a witch's tit out there,' Percy said, almost shouting because he was chronically deaf. He ambled up to the brazier with his hands held out. 'Either my blood's getting thinner, or the winter's gettin' worse.'

'You're gettin' old,' Clara said.

'Sixty ain't old.'

'Not to some folk, them as lives in nice warm houses an' gets regular meals. Fifty's pretty old when you don't have them things. Look at young Mary there. Eighteen, lookin' thirty.'

'That's because she's not well,' Percy said. 'She should be in hospital. I don't know how many times I've told you that.'

'She doesn't need no hospital. They only mess you

153

about in hospitals. Remember what happened to Terry, him as lived in this gaff before us? Went into hospital an' never came out.'

'He was old,' Percy said. 'Older than me.'

'I can look after Mary on me own,' Clara insisted. Since the day Mary had walked into the house Clara had assumed the mantle of motherhood. 'I'm just doin' her some nourishin' milk an' bread. That'll put the colour back in her cheeks.'

Percy grunted. 'It'll take more than slops to do that.'

Mary lurched and toppled sideways off the crate. She landed on her shoulder and rolled on her back before Percy could get to her.

'I'm bloody tellin' you, Clara,' he grunted as he helped Mary up, 'this kid should be in hospital.'

'She just nodded off, didn't you lovey?'

'Yeah,' Mary said, letting Percy help her on to the crate again. 'Dozed off, I reckon.'

It kept happening. She hadn't been dozing at all, she'd simply lost her balance. Balance was once something she took for granted, but not nowadays. It would leave her without warning; the room or the street or wherever she was would seem to tilt sideways and the next thing she felt was the pressure of the floor or the ground on her body. She had given herself a bloody nose on the waste ground outside the house one day, bending over to pick up something.

'I don't care what anybody says,' Percy muttered, 'a kid that's as sick as she is, an' carryin' a baby at that, ought to be gettin' looked after proper.' He leaned close to the fire again. 'This ain't the kind of life for her.'

'It's not done you or me any harm, has it?' Clara said.

'I can't say as it's done us much good, either.' Percy spat into the brazier. 'We didn't exactly have a choice. It

154

was either livin' rough, or bein' shut up in a bloody institution.'

At first Mary had thought Clara and Percy were married, but Clara had eventually told her they were brother and sister. Mary believed they were both alcoholics – they certainly got drunk most nights. When they were drunk they would talk about the days when they lived in a house, a proper house. It had been a very long time ago, Mary believed. They had been thrown out of their house because a time came when they had no money and were drunk more or less all the time. Mary thought it was a sad story; it was like lots she had heard since she left the tyranny of the nuns and began to wander from place to place, joining up with sullen bands of older people, listening to them filter their woes through alcoholic miasmas.

When Clara had finished preparing the milk and bread she stood over Mary and watched her spoon her helping out of the big enamel mug they used in place of a soup bowl.

'Take every drop, now. It'll put new strength into you.'

Mary managed to finish it. She handed back the mug and thanked Clara. 'It was lovely,' she said, although she hadn't been able to taste much. Nothing seemed to have any taste any more. And whenever she ate she became very sleepy. 'I think I'll go and lie down for a bit.'

'That's it, lovey.' Clara took Mary's arm and helped her across to the ruptured sofa that did service as her bed. It was damp and it smelled of mildew and something like old vegetables, but with a blanket over her Mary found it comfortable and warm.

When Clara had tucked her in she closed her eyes and let her mind drift. She thought of schooldays, days with the band, friends and enemies she'd had; she remembered the young man who had helped her to find the Catholic hostel, and she recalled wishing she'd at least brought his card when she ran away from there. She would have 'phoned him, because he had said he was there to help. And she had needed help so many times.

Drifting towards sleep she thought of her father. She sometimes longed to see him, but the thought of her mother always drove the longing out of her. She would see him again some day – some day when she wasn't so ill, and when she had her baby with her, his grandchild. Beneath the blanket she felt the firm lump at her stomach. It was twitching again. Mary wondered if it was a boy or a girl. She fell asleep wondering.

When she awoke, abruptly, sitting bolt upright, she couldn't tell where she was. It didn't seem like the room she had fallen asleep in. Clara was screaming and shouting and there was smoke everywhere. Mary began to realize that the odd light in the place was a fire. Something was burning.

'Stupid old bugger of hell!' Clara screeched, emerging wild-eyed from the smoke. 'Get up, Mary love! Quick, get up!'

Mary struggled off the couch. 'What's happened?'

'He's set fire to that can of petrol he's been saving! Dropped a bloody dog-end into it! I told him he shouldn't keep it indoors!'

Mary hurried to the door, past the burning can which had ignited a roll of old carpet and a leatherette armchair. 'Where's Percy?'

'Outside, tryin' to get some water.'

As Mary and Clara stepped into the open they were confronted by another odd light. It was blue and flashing and it was coming across the waste land towards them.

'Christ, it's the police,' Clara wailed. 'The stupid old sod's brought the law down on us.'

The next ten minutes were too hectic and confused for Mary to comprehend. A fire engine came and men in helmets began running all over the place with hoses and axes, while policemen tried to break up a gathering crowd of onlookers. Clara wailed endlessly and Percy kept shouting at the firemen to leave things alone and let him get on with his own business.

'It's only a little bit of fire, for God's sake! I can cope with it myself!'

Waking so suddenly had made Mary feel queasy. She moved away from Clara and bent over, trying to be sick. Somebody grasped her arm.

'Are you all right, love?'

Mary straightened and looked round. It was a young policewoman. 'I'm just feeling a bit sick, that's all.'

The policewoman frowned now, taking in Mary's appearance. 'Where do you live?'

Mary pointed to where the firemen were spraying water and using their axes. 'There,' she said.

The policewoman looked down at Mary's bulging stomach. 'You live *there*, in that old house?'

'Yeah.'

'That man and woman, are they your family?'

Mary shook her head. 'I just live with them.'

'Wait there, will you?' The policewoman walked away a few yards and began talking into her radio.

Waking again, she saw she was in a white room with white curtains and a white table by the bedside. The air had a smell, but this time it was of flowers, the artifical, not-quite scent of roses.

'How do you feel?'

157

Mary looked to her right. A woman was sitting there, complementing the room with her white coat. Mary tried to gauge how she felt. 'I'm kind of . . . I don't know. It doesn't feel like me.' The woman was easy to talk to. Mary didn't have to avert her eyes from the nice face, the friendly mouth. 'How long have I been sleeping?'

'Fourteen hours. Do you remember coming here?'

Mary thought. She remembered the fire, the police-woman and the ride in the police car. After that it was a jumble. A doctor had examined her and when he left her on the trolley she believed she must have drifted off to sleep.

'Is this the same place where the doctor saw me?'

'Yes. This is the King George the Sixth Hospital. You're in a side ward at the moment – you'll go into the main ward in a couple of days. My name's Ruth, by the way. Ruth Templeton. I'm a doctor, too.'

'Is there something wrong with me? Or is it just because I'm pregnant I've been feeling so odd?'

'There's quite a lot wrong with you. You're suffering from malnutrition, for a start. And you're anaemic. We're going to straighten all that out, and a few other things besides.' Ruth looked at a pad she was holding. 'We've got your name, Mary Smith, and that's all. Where does your family live?'

'I don't have a family,' Mary said, averting her eyes for the first time.

'Just as you wish.' Ruth wrote something and put down the pad. 'How long have you been living rough?'

'I'm not sure. Months, I think.'

'Do you know how long you've been pregnant?'

'No,' Mary said. 'I kept track for a while, but then I couldn't remember.' What she knew, but couldn't put into words, was that time had lost its continuity. Days never seemed to take her anywhere but back to where she started. 'Can you tell how soon it'll be before I have the baby?'

'A couple of weeks,' Ruth said. 'Maybe less.'

'What'll happen to me after I'm out of hospital?'

'Well, you've nowhere to live, no family, no money. So it looks like our best bet will be a State Welfare Home. They'll look after you until the baby's born. After that, the social workers will do what they can to find you a flat or a room somewhere.' Ruth paused. 'It's not going to be too easy for you.'

'It's never been easy.'

'No, I don't suppose it has.' Ruth stood up. 'Now you're awake, I'll get started on your medication.' She went to the door. 'I'm afraid that when I come back it'll be to give you a couple of injections. But don't worry, they won't be painful.'

When Ruth had gone Mary lay and stared at the spotless white door. She felt as if she had come out of a long tunnel into sunlight. She wondered if Clara and Percy had been taken away to be looked after, too, and if they were feeling the way she did.

She thought about the baby. It would be something of her very own. The more she thought about it the more she liked the notion of being a mother. Her baby would be her way of showing the world she could cope – because mothers were the ones who really coped, that was something everybody took for granted.

So she would have her baby, a bit of self-esteem, and a place of her own. *A place of her own!* The prospect was getting exciting. Shattered dreams, ruined hopes – none of them mattered. They left her with no regret. For all Mary knew the bad times might have been necessary, just to bring her to this moment and these prospects.

Ruth had said the time ahead wouldn't be easy. Compared to what she'd been through the past few years, Mary reckoned it would be a piece of cake. It would be a dream.

'This time, with a bit of luck, I'll be able to hang on to it,' she whispered, and gently patted her stomach.